To Geoff.

Best wishes to my reading mate.
Hope you like it

John

June 2002

John Lawson is a graduate of Leeds Metropolitan University in Psychology and Literature. He worked as a training consultant implementing profiling and diagnostic systems for people with learning difficulties. John has undertaken projects in Bolivia, introducing current concepts in teaching with Quechua and Aymaran peoples. After many discussions with Hugh Larkin it became apparent he could offer some new concepts to soccer aficionados.

Hugh Larkin is a graduate of Hull University in History and South-East Asian studies. He has lectured there and works as a freelance careers adviser. During a recent, quixotic journey through Eastern Europe in a 12 year old Toyota driven by a Danish soccer nut, he realised that some parts of soccer history are rarely told. After many discussions with John Lawson it became doubly apparent that concepts blended with facts become new possibilities.

GRANVILLE TINGATE

The Life and Times of a Yorkshire Football

John Lawson / Hugh Larkin

GRANVILLE TINGATE
The Life and Times of a Yorkshire Football

Vanguard Press

VANGUARD PAPERBACK

© Copyright 2002
John Lawson/Hugh Larkin

The rights of John Lawson/Hugh Larkin to be identified as authors of this work have been asserted by them in accordance with the Copyright, Designs and Patents Act 1988

All Rights Reserved

No reproduction, copy or transmission of this publication may be made without written permission.
No paragraph of this publication may be reproduced, copied or transmitted save with the written permission or in accordance
with the provisions of the Copyright Act 1956 (as amended).

Any person who does any unauthorised act in relation to this publication may be liable to criminal prosecution and civil claims for damage.

A CIP catalogue record for this title is available from the British Library
ISBN 1 903489 41 5

Vanguard Press is an imprint of
Pegasus Elliot MacKenzie Publishers
www.pegasuspublishers.com

First Published in 2002

Vanguard Press
Sheraton House Castle Park
Cambridge England

Printed & Bound in Great Britain

Dedication

To my son Tim - a great footballer and story teller.
Also to the man with the spirit in his eye.

John

ACKNOWLEDGEMENT

To Jen - for inspiration, encouragement, support, proofreading and occasionally falling out of bed laughing whilst singing ball chants.

- John

To all the people I have talked football with over the years.

- Hugh

Chapter 1 – The Pope

It was one of those nights that I will never forget – standing outside in hard driving rain, a cold wind tearing into my very bones. Feet wet and sodden through, and the only protection I had was a small plastic bag with a change of socks, knickers and T-shirt. I wanted to curl up and put myself into the bag for a couple of hours.

There I stood, waiting for my old friend Philip, in a shop doorway below his flat somewhere in Birmingham. It was late, 11.30 to be precise, and that wonderful friend of mine (who said he was going to leave a key under a plant pot on the outside landing) had forgotten me!! Where was he?

I was exactly a hundred and seven miles from home, wet and cold. Yet I had a faint glimmer of excitement still burning deep down because the reason for the visit was simple. Philip was a successful accountant from Oxford working for a well known sports paper and I fancied myself as a sports writer. I suppose it's in us all – that wish to make a statement and be appreciated. I suffered the typical normal family upbringing of the trials and tribulations of school, with parents that always know best. Well that's why we have friends I think, to share things and appreciate each other and take you as you are.

Anyway, Philip had invited me down to look at some of the ideas I had been working on and I had sent him down a floppy to look at three days earlier. Whilst I was waiting I wondered if he had read the contents yet? Well, I thought, he better had because I was freezing cold.

I started to think about the old days when a bunch of us

all seemed to live round the corner from each other. Everything was open house then; in fact we rarely locked the doors and certainly never locked the cars up. Mind you, they were such wrecks that nobody would ever steal them. Philip's boot was held together with rubber bands and I had a loose wire that was somehow connected to the electrics, which occasionally dropped to the road level underneath the main chassis of the car. I was told it looked like my Mini was powered by the biggest bonfire night rocket you could buy. Of course my friends never told me because they thought it looked good. Another friend who was a musician had the engine bits and pieces held together with guitar strings; in fact he always carried guitar strings in the boot in case of breakdown.

Well time went on, it was 11.56 exactly, and I said to myself in my serious mode, 'I'll give it until 12.10 exactly for Philip to turn up and if not, I will go find a cheap hostel or something'. I then started to rehearse lines like 'Some friend you are!' or with a bit of drama, 'I could have died of exposure!' or more simply, 'You fucking bastard!'. Then I thought, Philip likes a debate, therefore I should say, 'Philip, you must have had some pressures on you this week as I have tried to call to check everything is okay for me to come and got no reply. It's great to see you but honestly I'm frozen etc etc etc…'

At 12.05, I settled for 'You fucking bastard!'

I also started thinking about what I perceived to be Philip's weaknesses – like his obsession with hair gel and dangerous bondage; not that the sex part was dangerous, it was who he did it with, like the wife of a wrestler or the girlfriend of a local boxer. I then looked at my watch, waiting for 12.10 and on precisely the second the tenth minute struck, something strange happened – the rain stopped like a tap being turned off, and the wind became warm and gentle. I looked up and it was one of those skies that you love – you know, when it's gentle and warm on the ground, but when you look up the sky looks big and dramatic and everything seems like turmoil up there, with the clouds racing at seemingly hundreds of miles per hour. To me it was nature's cleaner going round very busily with a hoover that blows not sucks.

It was 'wonderful' to watch, using one of Philip's favourite words. I stood and allowed the steam to rise from my clothes and bathed in the glorious colours of blue in the night sky. There was even a part of the sky with that Van Gogh blue – if you ever get to Paris, go to the Musee d' Orsay and catch a few of Van's paintings: when you look at them you think, 'I've seen that colour or those colours and textures in special moments of real life'. Then it dawns on you that he does it like no other painter. Then you wonder at why other painters can't do that. By the way, no book can capture the impact and beauty of seeing a real live Vanny!

Well, time drifted and I was watching the water run down the sloped, cobbled street. Suddenly I got a 'stir of hairs on the back of the neck' syndrome as a rat ran out of the doorway that I had been sheltering in, ran into the middle of the street and perched on to a high cobble. It looked at me, looked up to Philip's flat window as if communicating with someone, and darted down the street. Now it wasn't the rat that made the hairs stand on the back of my neck; it was something else. I get these things happen to me from time to time. Not the 'I have met you before' or 'I have been here before' stuff but more that something is about to happen which will affect me for the rest of my life – you know, like Keegan signs for Newcastle or Clough buys Francis, yet I knew it was going to happen!

Well, the water in the road started to recede and at that moment my head was turned by some force to look at the moon – I soaked in its brilliance and then my head was forced to look down at the perfect round puddle that had formed in the middle of the road. The cobbles stuck out in the puddle like neat little hexagons and then the reflection of the moon appeared from behind a racing cloud and the puddle transformed into a perfect football. Amazingly the rat jumped into the middle of the puddle, perched on the highest cobble and looked up to Philip's window. Believe it or not, I was sure I heard the rat laugh, and then I heard a laugh from Philip's flat, and the laugh was one that I had known all my life, yet I knew I had never seen or met the being behind the laugh. The rat darted off once again.

Something magical was happening. I slowly moved into the middle of the road, bending over to get closer to the football puddle – and then all hell broke loose. A taxi came racing towards me, I fell in the puddle, the taxi swerved and mounted the pavement and at the same time sprayed me with water from the kerb edge. The taxi driver jumped out and in a typical Birmingham accent called me a 'cowin' pillock' – there were other insults but angry Brummies are even more difficult to understand than normal. He then grabbed my collar and just as I thought he was going to punch my lights out, a voice said,

"Bren, it's you – how are you?"

My initial reaction was, yes that's Philip, but how has he control over the taxi driver who froze when Phil spoke? Philip flashed a tenner at the taxi driver who almost doffed his cap, jumped into his cab and careered down the road. 'How does Philip do that?' I thought. At that point I was introduced to Philip's girlfriend of that evening (as I knew he didn't have a regular girlfriend). After pleasantries whilst they were trying to clean me up in the street and Philip's 'How long have you been waiting?' type questions, his girlfriend let out a real ripping scream and pointed to the middle of the road – it was my little rat. Without thinking I said, "It's okay. He's waiting for someone in Philip's flat and he's a real football fan with a sense of humour".

Philip turned me round so as to demand that I look at him whilst he looked at me. When puzzled, Philip never got angry, but would look at you and slowly contort his face, draining it of blood, and when nearly losing all self-control would open his mouth and change the subject as if nothing had happened. He always did this even if he walked into his old flat and flicked the light switch to find that the bulb had gone completely. He would stand a few seconds, go through his routine and then say something like, 'So tell me what happened with your cousin's mother who died of malaria?' We would then stand in the dark having a conversation until I would point out that we needed to change the light bulb. This non-acceptance of things created a trying time for Philip and myself later.

I was ushered up the outside stairs and deposited in his flat's front room, overlooking the street. I could see (I had not visited this flat before) that I was surrounded by Habitat's best furniture, all in pastel shades with walls to match, and an array of photographs on the walls of famous sports people and, not surprisingly, signed by the said famous people. And, as would be expected, the photos were smothered in kisses. I grinned to myself at the thought of being kissed by some of the athletic females (no names mentioned), then took it a quantum leap and further thought of being made love to by a female with enough bone and muscle to build and knock down the proverbial 'brick shithouse'. I then shuddered at the thought of my body being pounded to pulp and concentrated on what was happening and could not get it out of my head that someone listened to my thoughts and was having a little snigger.

"Well, Brendan, my friend," Philip said as he slid into an armchair, closely followed by his servile girfriend – I knew she was servile as she almost crouched as she walked, you know as though she was walking through a dark corridor with no lights and loads of cobwebs, yet maintained that simpering smile. "This is Catrina."

Philip gestured to her in a courtly manner.

"We have had a long day, so I am going to turn the heating up – give you a wonderful duvet and a full bottle of single malt whisky and we'll see you in the morning."

With that statement he jumped up and set off to get the said articles.

"Will you be alright in here?" spoke Catrina, whilst cocking her head to one side as though I was to pour the answer into her upright ear hole.

"Sure," I said looking out of the window. "I just hope my rat will be okay."

Catrina jerked and spun round.

"I'll just find Philip."

She set off to find him. A few seconds later Philip came back without Catrina and put the duvet on the settee, and whisky plus glass on the coffee table.

"Bren, I'm sorry about earlier, but I'll make it up to you tomorrow. Well, I'm off to bed – you stay up as long as you like; watch a video or something. We'll catch up on everything in the morning."

"No problem," I returned, and before I could pour myself a hefty glass of whisky, Philip was gone into his bedroom and I could faintly hear his 'I am a wonderful, caring, sensitive man but I simply have to shag you' voice-tones at work.

Well, let's move on. After two glasses of Highland Park single malt whisky and a quick look at the photos on the wall, I did a quick strip, put on dry knickers, socks and T-shirt, wandered over to the window and stared out at the still-wonderful sky. I felt like the master of all I surveyed because I was warm and glowing from the immediate effects of the whisky and couldn't care less who saw me dressed as I was, because it wasn't my neighbourhood. I went and sat down and looked back through the window and could just see the moon; I adjusted the settee so I could lay back with my feet on the coffee table and still see the moon.

Normally at the end of the day I like to reflect a little and sort out any issues of conflict so that I sleep well. My mother used to say, 'Never go to bed with bad thoughts and finish any arguments before you go to sleep'. I suppose things were okay, except me feeling a bit bitchy about Catrina. Next was to get my socks off without sitting up and without using my hands. I struggled a bit and nearly knocked the Highland Park over, when a voice came crashing into my head.
"CAREFUL!"
I sat up and looked round, to find only myself in the room and Philip was obviously occupied with Catrina. I focused my mind and was running through in my head what I was doing just before I nearly knocked the bottle over, when the voice said,
"Yes, I said be careful. Anyway, have you finished your

mental exercises because we need to talk seriously! By the way, bring the thought of Philip and the electric cupboard to the front of your brain – it is nearly there and it will have given you a laugh if you are slightly frightened at my voice. I'll shut up for a minute to let you process what's going on – also, it's a pleasure to meet you. Philip's been really good to me but you're the first ball psychic I've had in this room with me for two months."

I was in shock. I am not the type to shout, 'Come out you bastard', mainly because they might, and my strength is my brain not my fists, so I sat there not moving and processed again. For some reason my fear went quickly and I found myself thinking about the time when Philip got really pissed; we found him in an electric cupboard watching the meter go round, saying, 'I am going to make a determined effort to understand electricity this year – do you know that little meter? I'm talking to you. I think you are wonderfully constant and reliable in everything you do'. I grinned and thought, 'okay, let's get serious' and poured another whisky whilst trying to be incredibly brave.

"There are more wondrous constant things than electricity in this known universe," the voice said in a not-so-loud tone.

"Where are you?" I queried.

"On the window-sill," came the reply.

"Oh really!" I said, looking at the window-sill and finding that all I could see on it was a tatty old football resting on a plant saucer. My thoughts went out of the window thinking of the possibilities of someone outside.

"NO, NO, NO, I'm here on the window-sill. Look at the ball Look at me. I am the ball. I am the ball."

I suddenly got that feeling again like I've told you before – this one is going to be big. I stood up and walked slowly towards the ball.

"If it's okay with you," said the ball, "I'd rather you sit down over there whilst I talk to you, as you can understand the power you have over me in terms of you could throw me out of the window when I annoy you."

I sat down and laughed out loud. This is not happening, I sang to myself.

"Anyway," I blurted cockily, "why would I want to hurt you?"

"Because we are going to have very personal and tense conversations which may challenge you quite a bit." The voice had a serious tone now. "So stop playing with your sensory motors and you don't even have to talk if you don't want, because this is all thought transfer."

"Yes, but I could be inventing you," I said trying to convince myself that I'm really pissed now and getting worse than Philip in the electric cupboard.

"Okay. Let's go through the 3 p's – pleasantries, proof and possibilities. Firstly, I know your name because I often read Philip's mind; therefore I know a lot about you as he thinks of you often. Let me introduce myself. Granville Tingate is the name. Secondly, you will be wanting proof that I exist. So, in a moment I want you to ask me something about football that you do not know the answer to, so that tomorrow when Philip drops you off in the city centre you can go research the answer and find that I am totally correct and exist beyond doubt. Possibilities – ah yes, that's later when we start expanding our knowledge bases."

I thought hard. Is this still happening? Am I starting to get flu or something or shall I play along until I fall asleep?

"Well, I will still be here in the morning so fire away; you have nothing to lose but your personality and your future!"

Then silence fell and Granville was not in my head. I

could feel him not being there.

"Okay," I said to myself, "Here are six things I've always wanted to know about football and I will make them varied."

I thought and noticed some paper on the main table so I grabbed it and a pen and started making notes.

Two or three minutes later I had the questions and Granville was still not in my head.

"Are you there?" I asked and felt like a spirit medium – no reply.

"Are you there?" I asked again and thought, well that was different; no reply, ergo I will get back to the whisky and regroup my head and then have a nice sleep.

"Brendan." Granville came back into my head like a steam train. "Your fifth question is wrong because you already know the answer, so pick another one."

My head was mine again so I wrote another question double quick as though I was at school.

"There," I said. "I will read them out."

Granville replied with a condescending "if you must – but I already know what they are, don't I?"

"I want to read them out," I asserted. "Here we go:

1) Why are West Bromwich Albion known as the 'Baggies'?
2) Where is Port Vale?
3) Who was the first British player to be a big success in Italy?
4) How many England players have had a surname beginning with 'q'?
5) Which team is the worst ever to play in the football league?
6) When did leagues start outside Britain?"

"Good questions," stated Granville, "and here are the answers:

Number one. Now I know why you chose this one," said Granville knowingly, "because there's more than one answer to it."

"There is?" I mumbled.

"Of course. It's either because halfway through the first half, the blokes who collected the gate money had to carry it to the office at the other end of the stadium – hence the 'Bagmen'; or," Granville continued majestically, "it refers to the trousers worn by the many supporters from the local furnaces and ironworks; or it might have been taken from the big shorts worn by an Albion right-back in the early days. And the club was also called the Throstles. Funnily enough there are two explanations for…"

"I get the picture," I interjected. My head still throbbed and Granville seemed primed to go on all night about the folklore of the Albion.

"Second," continued the ball, in a tone that indicated that he couldn't understand anyone who wasn't fascinated by the WBA club history, "we come to Port Vale. It doesn't exist."

"Pardon?"

"The name Port Vale was taken from the house of a founder. The club started in Burslem, one of the towns of the Potteries. It was originally called Burslem Port Vale."

This explained a conversation I'd once had on a station with an irate Bury fan who told me that visiting Port Vale had been the most difficult away trip he'd ever had. Because he had to catch a train he hadn't finished the story of his journey; but now I understood. Not surprising that he had problems looking for signposts to the town of Port Vale.

Granville chimed into my thoughts. "Like Grimsby playing their home matches in Cleethorpes," he added.

"I know that one," I added irritably.

"Good. Well now we'll move on to Norman Adcock."

"Who the hell is Norman Adcock?"

"He played for Padova before the Second World War as a centre-forward. Pretty good too. Nearly ended up as capocannieri a couple of times."

"Alright, alright, is your name Granville or Glanville?"

We both knew what I meant. Brian Glanville, doyen of British soccer writers, had long had a distinct partiality to all things Italian and his work was peppered with liberos, catenaccio and brio – never use English if there's a Latin alternative, at least that's how it appeared.

"I'm just trying to be accurate," replied Granville sniffily. "We can do this another time if you want."

"No, no carry on. Sorry. I'm just not used to talking to footballs at this time of night."

"Very well. The only English international with a 'q' surname is Albert Quixall. Played for Man Utd. and Sheffield Wednesday."

My apology had been accepted but Granville seemed to have got the message because the rest of his answers were comparatively brief; even on the subject of the worst league team, which was a subjective question given the different numbers of games played, varying standards, inconsistency over a period against one season's disaster etc. Noting that I didn't fancy a detailed exposition, Granville settled for Loughborough Town in 1899-1900 in Div 2.They only won one out of 34 matches and because of this abject performance they failed to gain re-election and never enjoyed league status again. Apparently, the Swedes and the Belgians had their first league champions in 1896, pipping the Swiss and Italians who got in on the act in 1898.

"You can check all of those tomorrow; and any others you want to throw at me. I bet you never heard of Norman Adcock, eh?"

I confirmed to Granville that no, I hadn't heard of Norman Adcock, and he launched into a list of unknowns who were once famous. To make a point, I threw in Joe Waters who once scored twice in an FA Cup quarter-final on Match of the Day in the 70s, and Alan Seely, goal hero of West Ham's 1965 Cup-Winners Cup team, but Granville countered with a welter of obscure names and dates. I decided to concede to the ball's greater knowledge.

After that little debate I poured another whisky – bottle half empty now and I don't drink much. Anyway I thought, at least I'll sleep well.

"SLEEP WELL!" screamed Granville.

"Sorry," I said, "do you want to talk about your third "p" now – I think it was possibilities." But the word came out 'poshibililities'.

"I'll continue," said Granville. "As I said before, my name is Granville Tingate, ball of the stars, the ball with a bit of a reputation for expounding such stories that break all scientific paradigms and take you into universes that you have not thought of, and responsible for suppressing the epinephrine levels of many a football star to enable them to function best on the pitch and within your world!"

"Wow!" I returned. "I did not truly understand any of that but I'm sure you will explain…" I responded and slid further down the back of the settee to an almost horizontal position. "Let's start with something simple, like where did you get your name as you obviously weren't born with it?"

I reverted to my counselling skills and thought I'd better start at the beginning with this guy. I'll turn the gas fire down, I thought, and Granville came in to my head and said, "Good idea."

"Don't mention it," I returned.

"Not at all," big G said. God I've done it, I thought. I have given him a nickname already and that normally takes me months before I feel comfortable enough to do things like that with new people I meet.

"Don't like it," said Granville.

"Okay," I said.

"Okay," said Granville. "I chose my name myself. I was impressed with an old ball that I knew who allowed me to use his name. He was Granville Tingate and was a regular supporter at the Accrington Stanley football ground. I really admired his wit and story telling and thought someday I will be a legend like him."

I interrupted. "Accrington Stanley was the ground where the first penalty kick took place in 1893, scored by John Heath for Wolves."

"Yes, we know that, but do you know the name of the ball that played in that match? I do. It was Francisco Nadi, an Italian-made ball. Apparently in the early part of the century there was an influx of Italian immigrants. They came across with few worldly goods and with them thirteen balls arrived illegally. Out of the thirteen, two become involved in the first division by being in the right place at the right time and were picked up."

"Wow!" I responded. "I don't think that will get into a local pub quiz."

"Of course it could," laughed Granville – I recognised the laugh now – "if the contestants took a clever ball with them."

I suddenly had visions of pub quizzes opening with, 'Okay everyone, put your balls back in the cars and anyone found using thought transference will be excluded from the quiz'.

"Brendan." Granville sounded serious again. "Try to imagine what really happens out there in big league football with people that are ball psychic and a few knowledgeable balls."

"So tell me," I asked. "I really want to know!" I begged.

"Not tonight, Josephine," Big G said. "We will talk of possibilities and their real outcomes tomorrow when you are sober – by the way I've already told you I don't like Big G for a nickname."

"NO," I retorted. "I am interested because even though I have a reputation for having an above-average intelligence and have a photographic memory when it comes to sport, I suppose I don't ponder things enough. I usually cabbage out on the settee at home and watch television or read a good book – anyway, aren't books supposed to widen your horizons?"

"Yeah," responded Granville and I knew he was going to say something important because he went out of my head for a split second. "It depends on how you approach a book, soak it up and consider the possibilities. For example, you may consider it from a social-economic point of view or a post-modernist position; perhaps introduce Marxist analysis or take up a Hegelian position, or even the Confucian system."

"Okay." I was getting cocky now thinking of my university days of hours and hours of high level study. "We did all that at university as standard reading practice."

"I appreciate what you're saying, Brendan, but I'm talking about soaking it up, considering it and thinking of the possible outcomes for a few days and making notes BEFORE YOU READ IT."

"What." I jumped a little, well as high as you can jump

when being flat out on the settee – it was more of a sideways wobble. "That's ridiculous!"

"No, it isn't," responded Granville in a soothing tone. "Do this a few days before you read the book: guess what happens, make notes, and when you finally read the book two possibilities can happen. One, you have outshone yourself and predicted everything and more. Two, you are amazingly surprised as you have thought of all the permutations. This happens now and then and it is glorious. Look, Bren, millions of football fans do this every week. They discuss all the possibilities and turn up for the game and either walk away knowing that they understand the game well or are amazed and talk about it for the next week – simple, isn't it?"

"Okay, okay." I wriggled upright a little. "Let's consolidate." That's what I say when I don't know how to answer something.

"Consolidate what?" Granville exclaimed.

"Okay, okay." I squirmed, "I'll make a mental note of this."

Granville burst out laughing. "No, you will not. You always forget the things that can help you the most. And don't tell me you will write it down because you will lose it. Get a dictaphone – if you really are going to be a writer then get one. Here is something to motivate you – how many words can you hand-write in a minute?"

I thought hard and said, "About forty."

"No. Fifty-two point six is the average," Granville responded in a lovely 'I want you to remember this' tone. "Next question – how many words do you speak in a minute?"

"Fifty-two point three recurring," I said cockily.

"No, the average is one hundred and five and when you

are excited, it can shoot up to nearly one hundred and forty. I rest my case – get a dictaphone."

"Anyway," Granville continued, "just think, going back to book-reading possibilities, wouldn't it be great if school children had progressive teachers who gave out three classic school books and asked them to research the era etc., and come up with what they think the book should read like? Think of the motivation and learning and self esteem."

"Yeah," I responded glibly. "The teacher gives them Ploppy goes to London to consider and when the kids finally read the book, they become disillusioned because Ploppy finds that all the streets of London are paved with shit just like Ploppy. Anyway, you would need to have a union agreement in this day's present educational system. We couldn't have kids being more creative than their mentors now, could we? They would be in a position to print and design their own illustrations and possibly even market their books on the Internet. They would overtake all the adult writers within five years – now we could not have that, could we?"

I detected a bit of glee in Granville's voice- maybe I had tickled his fancy. "Well, I didn't like the Ploppy analogy but the second part has distinct possibilities for changing the education system. Very good, Bren, you are getting the hang of it now – nine out of ten, or better still would you like to mark yourself?"

"Fucking full marks." I slapped my leg.

"Stop swearing so much, unless it's positive or absolutely stonkingly funny."

"We all swear, especially football players who are paid well for it."

"Yes, I'll grant you that. Who are your top five swearers and why?"

I thought a while and started to warm to Granville because, even though he was starting to do my head in, he was interesting and seemed genuinely interested in my opinions.

"Okay, my top five and the reasons are: Ray Wilkins for being caught on microphone getting seriously shirty with a Chilean ball boy. Jack Charlton for his touch-line bust-up with the officials at USA 94. (I was aware that this had begun to sound like an Oscar nomination list). A surprise mention for Sir Alf Ramsay – that's for the time Sir Alf was at a game where the floodlights failed. When asked by a reporter how long he thought they would be off, the manager gave the withering reply, 'I am not a fucking electrician'.

"I'd go with Peter Reid of Everton who keeps up a choice line all through a game, and Graham Taylor and Lawrie McMenemy for the deluge they provided on that daft documentary."

"Okay," Granville responded, "but what about niño de la purta?"

"What was that?"

"Niño de la purta – it is Spanish for son of a bitch or worse depending on how you say it – you see you have not considered your answer. It should include all languages. For example, did you know that Goran Ivanisevic, the tennis player, makes a point of swearing in Croatian because umpires don't understand what he's saying? English is a tough language to use because most referees know a bit."

"Now if you're someone like Claudio Gentile you can go at it in Italian all game and a Dutch ref might not cotton on at all. Remember that match in Spain 82 when he took lumps out of Maradona and then Maradona retaliated and got sent off? Well, he was winding young Diego up all match, not just kicking him. When they asked him after the game about his cynical effort he just said, "No, senor, this is not dancing class."

"Even well-mannered guys like Jurgen Klinsmann are at it. Mind you, he has admitted swearing a lot, but he doesn't get caught because playing around Europe has broadened his vocabulary – he just picks a language the ref doesn't know."

"Then you get blokes like Cantona. Temper always on the edge, he'll just let it go at anybody. He got kicked out of one of his French clubs for calling his manager a "bag of shit" (in English) – then when he was up in front of a French FA hearing, they suspended him and he called them a bunch of idiots and he got a bigger ban."

"And then there's Welsh. A game between Abertillery Town and Fleur-de-Lys was abandoned because of bad language. The ref and linesmen couldn't stand it any longer. Best of all, an Italian was shown the red card in an amateur game in 1989 for dissent (i.e. swearing at the ref) and got so angry he ate the red card."

"Well," I slapped my leg again and laughed, "I'll be dipped in shit."

"There, you've sworn again."

"Oh, so you're the Pope now, are you?"

"Well no, I'm not the Pope but I reckon I've blessed more people individually than he has."

At that point I made the sign of the cross and grinned widely. Then I thought, I am a catholic and should not act like I am. I blamed the whisky, which was more than three quarters empty now.

"I have just worked out the possibilities and I think I am correct mathematically because where I come from in Yorkshire, it is common practice that when learning of mishaps, tragedy, sorrow and mistakes in daily life we say bless them or bless her/him. It just trips out naturally. I took this on board early and since I have been in my official office of ball of the stars for many years longer than the Pope, I could prove my case. Also there are times when we talk or gossip about people, especially their misfortunes, and it's almost like self-compensation for the guilt that we say bless'em to finish with – really what we are saying is "please bless me."

I didn't realise until Granviille had finished that I had been fingering my crucifix whilst Granville was talking.

"Give me a minute," I said to Granville and then fingered my own thoughts like rosary beads. "Okay, how do you like the Pope as a nickname?"

"Yes," said Granville, "I do like it and don't forget to use it when I'm gone."

"Gone," I said. "Where are you going? I've only just met you."

"Well, Bren, none of us are immortal you know."

"So tell me more about what you are and give me all the football stories and amazing facts."

"We will have plenty of time to start our mental journeys tomorrow. I think you should make that supreme effort and finish the bottle, turn over and have a lovely deep sleep. By the way, I hope you don't fart a lot because it seeps into my skin a bit like garlic and I could smell awful tomorrow."

"Goodnight then," I murmured whilst forcing down the last drops.

"Bless you," came the reply and he was gone from my head. My head was my own again. I tried to think but it was hard work. If this is all my imaginings then why is my head clearer the more drunk I get?

I laughed to myself as I thought, I have not named an

inanimate object since I named my teddy bear (I won't tell you what I called it). Also if people see a ghost or revelation they don't give it a nickname – they simply shit themselves. And why am I not frightened? All these questions, then my mind drifted. I sank into a deep sleep – and started to break wind loudly.

Chapter 2 – Philip will not meet the Pope

The next morning I was up and into the kitchen as I heard rumblings of breakfast. Normally I have been told that I walk a bit like a robot on acid, but this morning I simply cruised into the kitchen feeling great. Well, in truth I cruised slowly, but it felt like gliding. There was Philip looking absolutely brilliant as usual – hair gelled nicely.

"Morning, Bren," he said and stood up as though greeting a king, but he always did this and it always made you feel important. When someone calls for me I tend to open the door, not make any eye contact, turn and assume they are behind me – no conversation, and I usually head for the kitchen to put the kettle on, assuming that I am friendly and want their company. In fact I often leave people stood on the doorstep because I don't say, 'Come in'. In fact one person has got a self-esteem problem because of it – they would wait five seconds and walk away. But I suppose this goes back to my present work as a career guidance counsellor where they come to see me and I know they will follow me to my office.

Anyway, I slid into a chair in the most graceful manner and held a beaming grin across my face as wide as a kit-kat sideways.

"Morning," I smirked. "Good night last night with Catrina?"

At that moment, Uriah Heep of the glam world walked gently into the kitchen, put her arms round Philip's neck and whispered, "You're not a bad shag but I hope you haven't taken my simpering good looks away from me." Well, she didn't actually whisper those words, but that's how I processed it in my little brain.

"Brendan, Catrina's heading for France today to meet some friends, drink some champagne and generally mellow out," said Philip, stroking her thigh.

"Brilliant," I said. 'Hope you stay there,' I thought.

"Right," said Philip. "Let's get ready as Catrina will be catching a train soon. Then we'll go to my office at the paper, grab a coffee, and decide the plans for the day."

"That suits me," I responded and went to get a quick wash. When I'd finished I moved slowly into the front room where Philip and Catrina were putting their shoes on. I looked across at the window and the Pope was GONE!!!!

My response was immediate.

"Where's the Pope?" I asked in earnest.

"In the Vatican the last time I heard," responded Philip as though I was asking a genuine question about the Pope.

"No. I mean Granville Tingate?" I muttered as though it was obvious.

"Fucking hell, I didn't know that was his real name – are you on to something that I don't know about, Bren?" Philip always took everything I said literally.

I collected myself and said, "I'm thinking out loud, sorry. By the way, where's the ball off the window-sill?"

Catrina answered in that smug way, with a shuggle of her hips like a little prim and proper school child.

"Oh, Philip does this thing every morning where he opens the back kitchen window and kicks the ball out of the window as far as he can. He should do it more often – that's what balls are for."

After that she bent over to fasten her final shoelace; I looked at the well-rounded rear end and thought, 'I wonder how far you would go through the window'.

"Now you know that's not the reason, is it, Catty?" said Philip.

'Catty??' I thought, 'the sooner she stands up and takes away the temptation of me kicking her into St Andrew's the better.'

"The reason is, Bren, and you will understand, is that the ball likes to get out for the day as there is not much to do round the flat." I was shocked. So Philip is hooked up into this thing as well.

"Sorry about the Pope, Philip, as I gave Granville that nickname last night," I said in all innocence.

"Come again, Bren?" said Philip as he led us out of the flat. "What is all this Pope - Granville nonsense?"

I thought quickly as we were going through the flat door.

"Hang on, I need my wallet," I blurted; I ran back into the kitchen and strained my eyes to scan the garden - there was the Pope seated nicely under a tree. Well, I thought, I've got about two seconds for this. I strained my brain and thought as hard as I could of sending a message to the Pope in the garden – nothing. I strained again – nothing. Once more I thought and broke wind – nothing, nothing, nothing. Well, last night was a real freak of a night, I concluded. Yet at the back of my brain there was something about me writing down questions. I collected the paper off the coffee table because I wanted to know the answers anyway.

One last glance at the Pope – nothing. "Coming Philip!" I shouted and muttered something suitably Anglo-Saxon to annoy Granville. Immediately we were off into the centre in Philip's flash new car.

"This is nice," I said to Philip.

"Yeah," he said brushing his hair back with his hand.

"Which footballers do you think swear the most?" I

asked out of curiosity.

"Just about all of them, I'd say. Defenders are usually the worst though, and goalkeepers – especially keepers. They give their back four a real bollocking. Grobbelaar, he really gets stuck in. And Shilton just used to go spare if his defenders dropped back into the eighteen-yard box."

"No, you're not thinking right – what about niño de purta?" I said with an amazing Spanish accent and waited for a response.

"That was very good," Philip said. "Where did you learn that?"

"From the Pope," I said.

"Does he speak good Spanish?" said Philip.

"Well, I suppose so considering he comes from Yorkshire."

"Brendan," Philip got serious, "what do you know? Look, our paper pays well and we can even arrange a small advance just on a verbal statement – no questions asked."

"You kicked the answers to all this out of your window this morning," I couldn't stop myself from saying. Philip then went into his routine – blood drained from his face and then he went quiet and changed the subject.

"What are you doing tonight?" Philip aimed this at Catrina.

"That would be telling, wouldn't it?" said Catty in a ridiculous mother-type tone.

'Fucking hell,' I thought, 'I wish the Pope was here.'

We pulled up at Philip's office - private parking, I might add – and he whisked me upstairs and showed me the coffee machine. He then introduced me quickly to a female temp who looked as though she has been shagged by everyone in Torremolinos, and an outwardly gay guy who looked as though he shagged them all first and so was one step up in the hierarchy of the office.

"See you in twenty," Philip waved and slid through the door.

"Years?" I shouted and as usual he came back and said, "What, Bren?"

"Cheers," I responded and thought, 'you still fall for that after all this time.'

I looked around and thought, 'I can't stand hanging around here for two minutes, never mind twenty.'

"I'm just off for a wander," I shouted across to the young girl.

I darted downstairs, took a quick left and right when I got out of the building and ended up in a long road with houses down one side and railway lines on the other. I wandered across the road. There was a hole in the fence so I stepped through and saw a pile of railway sleepers; I skipped across two yards of weeds, sat, and started looking at a series of lines. I noticed that at the far side there was a road that ran along the other side of the last set of lines and about two hundred yards to the right it cut across to the road I was on. There was a set of railway barriers that go up in the air. I stared at the barriers. "Well this is exciting," I said to myself.

"Yeah, but a bit of patience and think what could happen – you know, the possibilities," a strong Brummie voice said. I looked around and there was nobody there!

"I'm over here," the voice said. I gazed through the weeds and just before my eyes met the track, there was a football.

'Oh no,' I thought, 'is this happening?' But it wasn't such a shock as last night. I plucked up courage and whispered, "Who are you?"

"Pongo Wareing at your service – look, he's coming!!!"

"Who?" I said, looking around me but seeing nobody.

"I told you. Over the other side. It could happen today. See the bloke riding the bike with his dog?" Sure enough there was a slightly overweight middle-aged man riding towards the barriers. At that moment the barriers came down and a car came to an abrupt halt immediately followed by a van which bumped into the back end of the car with that crunch of finality.

"See it could happen today – yes, he's going for it!" shouted Pongo.

I watched and saw the respective drivers starting to argue and at the same time the cyclist leaned his bike against the barriers and went to referee the two drivers. That's the thing about cyclists – always think they're so together just because they aren't using the earth's resources. There's still a deep strain of pacifism in the Liberals, even if they usually get their face filled in. 'Anyway, he was doing a great job' I thought; he didn't invade their space, used lots of smiles and open-handed gestures. I was straining to hear what was being said and Pongo screamed with laughter the way Brummies do – that child-like cheeky innocent type of laugh.

"LOOK AT THE BARRIERS." I couldn't believe my eyes. The bike was being raised by the barriers like a limp spider and the dog lead was fastened to the handle bars and the dog was on the other end of the lead with a glazed expression like it was being picked up by its mother.

I jumped up and screamed at the trio "THE BARRIERS" and pointed repeatedly. The cyclist ran to below his beloved dog and lifted his hands in to a position of prayer, looking up and shouting, "Jack, are you all right?" At that moment the barriers started to descend slowly – the signalman must have seen what happened. As the dog made its descent it was looking at its owner with a look of 'You twat. You stupid, stupid twat. How did you beat 10,000 other sperm?' The dog landed gracefully and within seconds everyone had disappeared on their way.

"See, I told you – I've been waiting for that to happen for fourteen months, two days and three hours," Pongo said smugly.

"What?" was my only response.

"Well, now we can have a chat – as I said, that man comes down there four times a day and he always seems to get the barriers down so it was a possibility that that might just happen and I worked it out – excellent, excellent. Anyway who are you and what balls do you know personally?"

I looked at my watch and thought, 'I can't explain this to Philip and must go.' I felt relieved that I had made the decision to go really quickly because my head was not mine again.

"I'm off," I said and started walking away briskly.

"Bye then," shouted Pongo. "Do you know anyone that I do?" was his last pitch at me.

"Only the Pope – Granville Tingate," I threw over my shoulder as my feet picked up speed.

"Ah the ball of the stars. I've heard of him – the Pope. A good nickname, eh?" His voice faded at the end and my head was immediately clear.

I bounced upstairs to find Philip in his office chair, smiling as I walked in.

"Nice little stroll then?"

"Yeah." I thought of the dog and laughed inside; that dog's expression – 'you twat, you stupid, stupid twat.'

"Philip," I asked, "whilst we're here, can you see if you have some answers to these questions I wrote down last night?"

"Yeah, sure." He started up his workstation and wiggled his fingers across the keyboard.

"Okay, answer one. There's loads of stuff on that Baggies nickname."

He confirmed all the details Granville had passed on about West Brom and the details of Port Vale's founding name. Looking up Loughborough's record was a bit more of a problem and he grumbled a bit because he needed to fetch a couple of fact books for this. Albert Quixall he already knew because it had come up in an inter-office quiz once. When it came to Norman Adcock his reaction was the same as mine.

"Who the fuck is Norman Adcock?"

"Played for Padova before the war," I replied calmly.

He grumbled and dug up some stuff from Channel 4 Italian coverage. There was a look of surprise on his face when the name came up.

"Why did you want to know that?" he asked.

"For a friend. He's always full of himself and I want to pull him down a bit," I lied.

By this time Phil was getting into it and he threw in some extra details. Port Vale nearly reached the Cup Final as a Third Division side in 1954. They were beaten in the semis by, of all teams, West Brom with a very hotly disputed goal. And West Brom's first ever game was against a team called Black Lake Victoria. On the topic of crap teams he threw in Stoke City's 1984-5 First Division campaign when they lost 31 out of 42 games and only scored in 17 games. Popular facts with Port Vale fans anyway.

"Just one more question, Phil. Have you ever heard of

anyone round here called Pongo Wareing?"

Phil laughed and said, "Bloke who played for the Villa years ago."

"Okay, Bren," Phil said as he stretched his back whilst sat in his chair, "what do you want to do tonight? I see we have two options: one, go to Spark Hill for a Balti then go home and get pissed, or two, go home and I will cook you something and then we get pissed. Which do you fancy?" My immediate response was to go for a Balti.

Whenever I hear the word Balti I always think of the first time Phil took a gang of us for a curry in Spark Hill. Phil took us in his old car and as we pulled up I'll never forget the image of a typically run-down area; just like in any city, the type of place you would not park your car for ten minutes. However, Phil said it was safe because there was private parking. Anyway we pulled up in front of the restaurant and this tall Indian guy walked across. He looked just like Michael Jackson with the military-style uniform in deep blue with gold epaulets, a pair of sunglasses and a military hat. He said hello and welcome to the restaurant and asked us to park opposite on a piece of waste ground. I muttered something about it being safe and Phil assured me that he was good.

I wasn't so sure. So we parked up and crossed back over ready to go into the restaurant. Just then our uniformed friend jerked his head to gaze across the road, then in one movement picked up a small pebble and sent it like an exocet missile across the road, skimming all the cars at high velocity. It hit the bicycle bell of two young thugs, ricocheting off and landed spinning circularly downwards inside a dustbin with incredible acoustics, making a deep grumbling sound. Everyone in the street saw it and was amazed.

Phil said smugly, "I told you he is good!!"

That wasn't all that night. Apart from the food being excellent, Jack, one of our friends who was a drummer, had never had a curry before. Also at that restaurant you did not get knives or forks so you had to use Nan bread or Chapatis. We were brought a 'compliments of the house' sauce, which was incredibly hot, with a little salad. Well, with the room being warm and Jack not having had hot food before, he broke into a sweat and the next thing to arrive was a layer of Chapatis that were bigger than normal. Jack assumed that they were face towels and proceeded to mop his face with one. He made a meal of it, wiping his neck, brow and giving the back of his neck a good rub. Then, neatly folding it up and laying it on the table next to his plate, he said, "The towels are lovely and soft here, I wonder what they wash them in?"

"Flour!!" I chirped whilst bending double.

"A hot frying pan with no oil!!" came out of Phil's mouth with a splutter.

Jack was confused...

"Sorry Phil," I said coming back to Phil's options. "I was just thinking of Jack – you remember the first time we went to Spark Hill?"

"Yeah, they were good times. Have you seen anything of Jack since he moved?"

"No. The last I heard was that he went for his 'once every three years' job interview and was with four others – they were given a little group chat before the individual interviews. Apparently the person interviewing went round the group and asked them their IQ. The first four were answering things like 105, 98, 115 etc and then Jack answered, "Mine's only twenty-two, I think!" at which point the interviewer responded to Jack with, "So, what size drum sticks do you use?" and laughed at Jack.

"Whoops," said Phil, "he did the wrong thing."

"Yeah, but apparently the interviewer did not spend a long time in hospital – and I haven't heard about drummer Jack since."

"Well, what do you want to do?"

"You cook in, and I can read you some of my work." I wanted to speak to the Pope.

"Sounds good to me. Let's go shopping."

During the quick whiz round the shops, I shot into an electrical shop and bought a dictaphone; Phil patted me on the back when I came out, saying, "Getting serious are we?"

We landed back at Phil's flat. We dumped the shopping in the kitchen and Phil said, "Do you fancy a red wine or beer before the meal?"

"A can will do me fine."

"Right, well I need space to get things prepared so do you want a walk in the garden to fetch my football in?"

"Excellent," I said, looking at the Pope. "Give me a shout if you want anything doing."

I sauntered into the garden and gave the Pope a long look. He was still there next to the tree. He had not changed position but I got the feeling that when I saw him earlier, before we went out, he was looking at the road behind the fence. I don't know how I felt this, as he has got no eyes. Yet now as I walked slowly towards him I felt as though he was looking at me.

"Quite right, Brendan. I was talking to Peter Withe in the street and it was of a personal nature so I screened everyone else out of the conversation. How are you today? Ready to carry on working on the 3 p's?"

I leant against the tree and collected my thoughts. I could feel Granville waiting for me and had three big swigs of the beer.

"Okay, you knew the answers, I'll grant you that, but Phil added a couple of things that you might not know, like…"

"Excuse me," said Granville. "Proof!!!! Are you happy now or do you want more?"

"No, I'm going to run with this while I am still sane and see where it goes. Anyway, I met another ball who has heard of you."

"Who was that?" interjected the Pope with great interest in his voice.

"Pongo Wareing," I replied as a matter of fact and feeling quite smug.

"What did he say?" screamed the Pope.

"Pongo said that he had heard of you as the 'ball of the stars' and thinks your new nickname as the Pope is brilliant."

"What was he doing and where did you find him, and by the way don't use nicknames lightly because they spread like wildfire. We'll have a conversation about nicknames later but as an example I once had an owner whose brother thought he saw the dead body of a young woman in a white dress face down in a canal. When the police arrived, after he had alerted them, there was a crowd. When they pulled what was thought to be a body out, it turned out to be a dead seagull with a wide wingspan. His last name was Simpson and someone there who knew him shouted out 'Seagull Simpson' and the name stuck. He has a bread shop and all the locals call him Seagull to his face – in fact I would think that it has gone on that long that no one knows his real first name now. I have been in his head many times and he goes through pain every time he hears the word Seagull. A lifetime of misery."

I considered what he said for a moment and then thought about how I had met Pongo. I told the Pope of what happened and the Pope said sadly,

"Do you realise how many balls are left abandoned all over the world. Railway sidings are common for leaving an unwanted ball. Sometimes intentionally and especially by railway lines when a group of football fans get drunk and throw them out of the train window – but we will talk of this later when I give you your lessons in ball truth!!"

"I'm going to get lessons?" I started to think that my life would not be my own soon.

"Your life is your own," the Pope retorted, "but you've connected with me and unfortunately we will always be together spiritually; it's my duty to give you all my knowledge, which is not just facts about football history. Yes, we are going to stick together one way or another, or as you would say, like snot hanging on the end of your nose when your hands are full."

I looked round the garden to ease the feeling of a full head, walked to below Phil's window and motioned for another beer to be thrown down. I walked back to Granville, downing the second can before I got to him. I then arrived at the tree and looked at Granville and let out a large belch. I started to talk to Granville and just as I was getting going again, a little boy popped his head over the fence. His head was vibrating; I saw the tips of his fingers over the fence-top going white and realised that he must be hanging on.

"That was a loud burp," he said, looking round. "Who are you talking to?" He carried on shaking a bit more and straining his neck a bit more to find only Granville in the garden with me.

"The Pope," I replied looking directly at and touching Granville gently with the end of my shoe.

The boy looked at me just like the dog coming down from the railway barriers and let go of the fence. He disappeared as fast as a computer screen when it crashes.

I expected a reappearance but he did not come. The Pope started humming to himself,

"Oh dear, oh dear."

"What's wrong?" I said, knowing that I had done something out of line again.

"Suit the situation," he said with a stern voice. "Being sensitive is a waste of time if you use this skill at the wrong time. Just think, every interaction requires a response and that response is sometimes based on experience of the situation and sometimes is an educated guess – that's where probabilities come in. but you just did something that was inappropriate."

"Go on then, I'm lost." I started to feel small and could feel a bit of tension. I was getting angry.

"Well, Bren, I am a football. Do not touch me lightly, my friend, as you insult me. To use your vocabulary, give me a good kicking; that's what I enjoy!"

I looked, I thought, I considered. Then I said, "Niño de purta," just like Andoni Goichochea, the Butcher of Bilbao, might shout and gave the Pope such a kick that it sent him right down the garden, smacking against the wall below Phil's kitchen window. I ran to get the rebound and whacked it; jumped up and caught the next rebound on my head; I was merciless. I chased and booted, giving the Pope no time to gather himself.

"Niño de purta," I screamed at the top of my voice as I spun and angled one into the corner, making the Pope wobble round the dustbin.

"Wheeeeee!" I heard the Pope say. "C'mon, you've got more than that!"

"Right!" I shouted whilst pointing my finger at him, "you'll love this."

I proceeded to volley shots at an incredible speed, straight in and straight back off the wall, getting shorter each kick. I was getting closer and harder till I was only six feet off the wall, creating a hard rhythmic crack against the wall.

"Wheeeeeeee!" screamed the Pope.

"You like it, don't you – you really like it!" I screamed.

"BRENDAN!!!" Phil shouted from out of the kitchen window. "Who are you talking to and more importantly who the fuck do you think the ball is? You're kicking seven bells of shit out of it."

I stood looking up at Phil, panting; and in a happy out-of-breath type voice said, "I'm talking to myself – giving myself the first lesson in ball truth, and kicking the shit out of the Pope. Okay?"

Phil's colour drained and he lurched back and slammed the window shut.

"Many thanks for that," said Granville.

"I'm kernackered," I said. "I'm off in for a few minutes. See you soon – and can you switch off to give my head inside a break?"

"Certainly – gone now!" and he was gone.

I staggered up the stairs and slid into the chair next to the kitchen table.

"Sorry about that, Phil. I got carried away."

Phil said nothing and continued cooking so I watched and laid the table.

We had a good meal and a good chat about the floppy I

had sent him with my work on. We threw ideas around. Phil expressed his concern in my odd behaviour. I knew then that Phil would never meet the Pope.

After a couple of hours chat, Phil suggested we move into the lounge, as he calls it, so I fetched Granville and agreed that we would speak later when Phil had gone to bed.

We had been sitting in the lounge for about ten minutes when Phil told me he had prepared what he called a perfect day - he had got two tickets for the Villa-Newcastle game the next day. I was excited. Just then the phone rang. I answered it as I was nearest to the phone. It was Catrina.

"Give me Philip, please," came the voice of authority.

"Hang on," I said thinking of a cliff with a sheer drop of two hundred feet.

"Oh sorry, Brendan, before you go, how are you?"

"I've just been told by Phil that tomorrow we are going to have a perfect day – what do you think to that?" I responded whilst just completing my vision of her landing on the beach like one of those crazy bastards that jumped off cliffs with hopeless birds' wings.

"Great," she said. 'What am I missing?' she thought, but did not dare say it.

"Here's Phil," I said putting an emphasis on PHIL as she would never call him that.

The phone was a walkabout job so Phil slid off into the bedroom to talk with Catty!

I sat and thought about a perfect day. Granville shot into my head. "Could we have a word before Phil comes back?"

"Sure, just give me a second." I wanted to think about Catrina's perfect day – what would it be like?

I started to go through her perfect day. 'Get up at seven with the sun streaming through the windows. Jump out of bed onto the scales to find I have lost seven pounds. Ring my best friend to find she has put on seven pounds. Have a voucher come through the door for a free total facial and hair-do at the best in the city. Find another personal invitation to the latest fashion show. Buy everything fashionable for this month. When walking to the chauffeur driven car, look like I've spent more than anyone else that day whilst managing to look as though the bags are a mental burden to me. Finish the day watching TV in my nightie after a hot bath – to find that all the clothes programmes are talking about everything I have just bought.'

I sniggered at myself and thought, 'what is my perfect day? Quite simple: Wake up and fart loudly. If I have female company, a blow job. Go for a shit. Slap-up fried breakfast. Another blow job. Football match. Few pints. Take-away curry, and to finish the day, make a fart that lasts for twelve seconds that would send the smelliest dog out of the room looking at me in disgust. My perfect day.'

"Brendan," came a whisper from Granville. "We must talk quickly – I must go to that match with you tomorrow."

"What for?"

"To see if there is anyone I know – to enjoy the game – to show you how it really works – to give you an edge"

At that moment Phil walked back into the room and the Pope was gone from my head.

"Let's talk about tomorrow," I said, as I opened a really good quality red wine. I hoped Phil would get drunk quickly on this then I could spring the question on him.

"Yeah tomorrow – I think it'll be a real cracker. Since Keegan took over at St James' they've played good stuff; plenty of guys who can knock it."

I knew that 'knock it' was Phil's ultimate accolade. He'd picked it up from the Liverpool of the 1970's who revelled in 'knock it and go, pass and move' etc. Abbreviated to 'knock it', the phrase had the air of nonchalance and style that characterised the best pros. It was also endlessly flexible – players could knock it in, knock it forwards, give it a little knock and much more. In some of his early reporting Phil had earned the editor's wrath for too much use of knocking. Betting on the number of times he used the phrase was a useful antidote to a boring game; I decided to encourage him a little.

"So you reckon they can play a bit?"

"Yeah. They're pretty committed to attack but with Peacock at centre-back I would be. Bloody traffic bollard he is."

"Bollard?"

"Pass on both sides. Anyway the midfield's got Beardsley and Sellars. They can both knock it. Then there's Albert. Interesting defender, good on the ball, brings it forward, and…"

"He can knock it?" I suggested.

"Right," said Phil nodding vigorously.

We spent a fair amount of time comparing the merits of the two sides. Phil was especially keen on the presence of two ex-Liverpool stars on the Villa side. Needless to say they both got a glowing reference for their priceless ability to 'knock it' and keep it simple – another key attribute in Phil's ideal team. I wasn't too bothered about the finer points, as both teams have always been fairly high in my estimation. I mean, there are some teams that you just never like; Leeds, Arsenal, Everton – no matter who they play, it's just such a fundamental thing even though the reason you hate them comes from way back. But none of these irrational feelings clouded my view of tomorrow's game, so I could go to sleep looking forward to a classy game, banter with Phil and Granville's contribution.

We had finished the wine.

"Well," I was ready to spring it on him, "can I take your football to the match tomorrow?"

"You can't take a ball to a football match," Phil sneered.

"Where else would it look in place – in a Turkish bath?" That was my first attack.

"Well, they search you."

"Oh yeah." I got fired up. "In your paper you could write 'Man fined at football match – in possession of a ball – how dangerous!'"

Phil put on his serious voice. "Bren, did you know that it is a fact that the police once banned Bristol Rovers fans from taking Weetabix into matches at Shrewsbury because they threw them at the Shrews fans?"

"Okay, let's talk about banned objects from matches – guess what got banned at Gillingham once?"

"Graham Taylor?"

"Close. Kent Police reckoned that celery was a 'threat to stadium security' so they confiscated it from the home fans. But that was in the bad old days when the fuzz thought everyone was a potential hooligan. I mean they don't stop Hereford fans taking their Swedes into a game now, do they? And every place Gazza goes, they chuck Mars Bars on the pitch. Someone once threw a lump of red meat in front of Tommie Smith so no one's going to worry about a ball, are they?"

"And don't forget Brentford fans and their cheese," added Granville.

"And what about Brentford and cheese," I repeated.

"Alright, alright, just give it a rest, okay? Christ, I bet the current definition of anorak in the Oxford English just says 'see Bren'."

Phil told me I was getting strange but he was still glad to see me. He then retired to bed.

"Is that okay?" I quipped at the Pope. "You're going to the match tomorrow."

"Fucking fannytastic!" screamed Granville. "Look, you get to bed – yes, I know I just swore but wait till you see me in action tomorrow – you won't regret it," and he was gone.

I smiled and thought, 'I hope you don't show me up tomorrow – but think of the possibilities and boy, am I going to have an edge on everyone in the stadium.'

Chapter 3 – The Big Match

I woke the next morning to the sound of someone singing loudly…

"SIMPLY THE BALL
DA DA DA DA
BETTER THAN ALL THE BALLS
DA DA DA DA…"

"What's going on?" I said, expecting Phil to answer.

"PRETTY BA-ALL BOUNCIN DOWN THE STREET
PRETTY BA-ALL THE KIND I LIKE TO MEET
PRETTY BALL DON'T BOUNCE AWAY FROM ME
YOU'RE ALL I SEE
MERCY…"

"Granville! What the hell are you doing? My head's exploding!!!"

"Sorry, bud, I'm on a roll – and we'll shove it up their arses today," he said in an American accent.

"My god, you've changed!!!"

"Okay, my little chicototo, un abrazo y beso – que tal?" He now sounded South American.

"What?"

"Okay, my little son, a hug and a kiss – how are you?"

"Calm down. I didn't know you were going to be like this." I was trying to clear my brain.

"Okay, I'm settled now." He went back into his sober voice. "It's been a long time and I was just regressing into the past a little. Don't worry, be happy – that could be a song one day," he laughed.

"Right, it's switch-off time while I get some breakfast," and he was gone.

I mooched delicately over to the kitchen and heard Phil come out of his bedroom. I put the kettle on.

"Mornin, Phil."

"Morning, Bren – you've put the kettle on. Gerate!!" I forgot that was another of Phil's favourite words – great but he made it sound like Tony the tiger, the one off the breakfast adverts.

"Want some toast?"

"Yeah, good idea."

With that, Phil sat down and looked at me with a really glowing smile and said, "Come on then, tell us what's been happening in the world of the career officer since I saw you last?"

It seemed like so long ago since I arrived, but I knew what Phil wanted. He didn't want to know about the political or departmental changes; he wanted a story…

I thought for a moment and said, "Well, I had this young guy called Pete Smith. About two weeks ago he came in for interview preparation. He was a great young guy but sometimes lacked confidence. Anyway I rang up a shipbuilder about fifteen miles out of town and arranged an interview for him at ten the following day. I didn't think anymore about it until the next day. Shortly after dinnertime he arrived in my office with tears in his eyes, and this was his story. He apparently turned up on his motorbike, to save on petrol, and went into the interview room to face a panel of four in his motorbike gear."

"That's a bad mistake," said Phil thinking about his dress code.

"No, it gets better," I said. "His confidence went and they asked him to sit down and he didn't take his crash helmet off – in fact he didn't even lift the visor up."

"That's brilliant!" says Phil.

"No, it gets better – after about five questions the interviewing panel could not hear a thing Pete was saying. Stuffed in his jacket was one of those portable radios that are very small but very loud – he accidentally knocked the 'on' switch and Radio One came blurting out with Satisfaction by the Rolling Stones. Shortly after this they shook his hand and told him they would let him know."

"Excellent," nodded Phil in approval of the story.

"No, it gets better because when he talked to me I asked him for the new address he and his parents were moving to (he told me before). Okay, I said. You're going back but this time as a different person – on the train – in a suit – with questions ready, etc etc. I rang up the company and told them it was a different Pete Smith – as they had never seen him, they said okay, tomorrow. So he went the next day, walked in dressed smart, gave them all a firm handshake, answered all the questions and asked a few himself at the end."

"That's really nice," said Phil nodding even more.

"No, I haven't finished yet. They offered him the job there and then, and then said to him that they had the most stupid prat the day before in a crash helmet with the radio blaring Satisfaction. Pete was asked 'I hope you're not going to be like him'."

Phil approved of that one and offered me another coffee.

"Oh c'mon, Bren, let's have another." So after a couple more, we got ready to go out.

We took the bus into town because we knew we were going to have a pint or two on the way and on the way back. Granville seemed happy in a plastic bag. He mentioned when we set out that he would not interrupt until the action started.

We fell into the Villiers Arms, quite close to the ground, for a pre-match dram. It was thick with smoke, beer and the talk of soccer. We edged our way to stand next to a table near the door. I placed Granville on the table edge and had a few quips with Phil about the game's outcome.

"So do you think Newcastle are going to knock it today?" I asked innocently.

"Ye-es, they've got the skill, they're unbeaten this season and you don't win at places like Highbury without talent and bottle," he replied. Phil's eyes narrowed as he suspected a piss-take. I carried on quickly and he couldn't quite decide if I'd been winding him up or not.

"My first chance to see Cole in action live. And Albert – I didn't think we'd ever see foreign players like that playing over here."

"Tremendous, just what we need. Get 'em all in. Kick the Brits out."

He was only half joking. For many years Phil had extolled the virtues of the game as played in Italy, Spain and all points of the compass, while bemoaning the lack of skill and technique in Britain. For a 12-year-old whose school bag had proclaimed the virtues of the ultra-defensive Inter Milan, the sight of top internationals making a living on Tyneside, in the North-West and Leeds was a dream writ large. The 1994-5 season promised to be Phil's Annus Memorablis.

"Well, there is Beardsley," I pointed out. I suddenly felt like I ought to defend the British game even though I shared a lot of Phil's opinions.

"Good player," he conceded. "It's all the better because Man U let him go when he was a kid." Like a true Liverpool fan Phil took pleasure in anything anti-United. "He had to go over to Canada to get a start. Typical of the English game."

He was off again and I always had worries when he got on to this subject – especially in pubs. Half-heard conversations of a slick-looking journalist (and Liverpool fan) criticising all things Brit on match days tended to excite the locals.

There were a group of men, young and old, sitting at the table, who were obviously interested in our conversation and one piped in. "You two reporters then? Can yo give us inside information loike?"

Phil replied coolly as he loved to elevate himself now and then. "I don't think the Villa will get much change out of Keegan's lot today. Allan Evans didn't seem too confident the other day. They don't know whether to man-mark Beardsley or not and there's a bit of concern about Staunton's knee."

Just as Phil finished, one of the young men grabbed Granville and opened the bag, just out of curiosity I suppose, but I couldn't help myself

"Keep your hands off the Pope," I said with a firm voice and reached to get Granville back. He laughed and passed it to his friend, saying, "It's only a fucking ball!"

Well what happened next was all over in two minutes but it seemed longer as it happened.

"It's only semi-good looks on your face but you want to keep them, don't you?" I said, getting hot under the collar.

"Well, we've got a reporter who is a hard case who wants his ball back actually."

'He sounded like a twat' I thought, with that irritating habit of adding 'aktewerleee' at the end of sentences to try to sound important. I like Brummies but that affectation really gets under my skin.

At that point they threw Granville across the room to some other supporters they knew. But it was too late.

Something happened to my normally 'run away and save my arse' survival approach. I jumped across three tables and walking across the top, I knocked over at least ten quids worth of beer and landed in front of the man with the ball. He was shocked and in a state of disbelief at my speed then received an incredible upper cut from me that lifted him fractionally. He then slid down the wall, at which point I grabbed the plastic bag and turned, thinking my job was done. I looked across and the tables were all being vacated. Phil was being surrounded by an angry tribe. I took a different route back – this time knocking over fifteen quids worth of beer and punched and chopped taking care of three holding Phil; they were left still standing but as zombies. I threw Phil out of the door and pulled the zombies in front so I was in between them and the door – by this time there was a heaving mass moving to my side of the pub. I quickly jumped up onto the chair nearest the door, spun Granville round in his bag, shouted, "GRANVILLE TINGATE – BALL OF THE STARS!" – did a quick spin and shot through the door to find Phil had done his job finding an escape route; he was sat in a taxi with the door open ready. I dived into the cab, Phil shouted, "tenner to get us out of here!" and the driver put his foot down.

Three blocks later Phil and I were walking down the street. Phil spoke for the first time since the pub.

"Bren, I know what happened and thanks for the help, but where did that come from? The aggression and speed. I mean it was awful to see you like that but, at the same time, I feel elated as though we've just won the war."

"I can't say," I replied. "I think that's always been in me but I didn't know I could do that kind of stuff."

"You didn't do it all by yourself, you know." Granville spoke for the first time in two hours. "I hooked up to your subconscious and made you process all your physical responses through your hypothalamus – this gave you those split-second edges."

"Fucking hell!!!" I exclaimed, thinking of the potential.

"What?" said Philip looking around expecting more trouble.

"Everything's okay, Phil, I was just thinking."

I patted Granville affectionately and put a big smile on my face.

Phil said, "I knew we shouldn't have brought the ball."

"This is just the beginning," I responded.

We called in at another pub that was full of old age pensioners – no bother.

Then off to the match we went. Phil had not told me that he had arranged for us both to be in the press box. So it was brilliant to be introduced to the real reporters. Phil knew most of them and went into journalist-speak very quickly. It was like another language – blokes taking about the editor needing 'four pars', 'trying to get a line to the subs' and asking who was on copy and so on.

I stared out of the press box onto the pitch. Newcastle had taken all their ticket allocation and turned their end into a mass of black and white. Somehow it looked colourful. Sales of replica shirts went through the roof the moment Keegan started bringing a bit of success back to the club and now they were back at the top of the Premier for the first time in God knows how long. A full chorus of the 'Blaydon Races' was in progress and the Villa fans in the Holte End were giving it full voice too. Just as well this wasn't one of those grounds with an open-air press box.

I took Granville out of the bag, positioned him at the end of the reporter's desk and took my end seat with him, overlooking the east end of the ground. He then spoke.

"Bren, you must do what I tell you when linking up to balls or you will go mad very quickly."

"What do you mean?" I whispered.

"There are about thirty balls out there in total and they all have something to say – it could be a bit much for you. So, when I tell you to switch to me, you must concentrate on me only. At this moment and since we entered the ground I have put up a screen around you – to protect you," he said in a grave voice. "Now that you are ball psychic you can talk to or hear any football but it can be overpowering. Let's do a quick test – I am dropping the shield now…"

A thundering noise of screams, voices with all different characters came flooding into my head and it amplified to such a point that I started to drop my head and put my hands over my ears. It was so loud and clear, like when you wake up from a dream after someone in the dream has shouted loudly – but twenty times stronger. I could hear Phil speaking to me with a distant voice, as though he was somewhere outside of the ground.

"Are you okay, Bren?"

I looked at Granville for help and all went quiet. "Don't worry, if we switch on and off for two or three minutes you'll get the hang of it. And every time you look at me for help just see me with a big help sign stuck on me and imagine it will be quiet in two seconds and it will!"

"Okay," I said.

Phil interrupted again. "Bren, are you alright?"

"Yeah," I said holding my head with one hand.

Then Danny who was the real reporter and colleague of Phil quipped, "It's too much for him – the crowd – the noise."

Granville gave me a quick message. I laughed and said to the reporter, "Didn't you know? I'm psychic and I've just found out what Keegan has said to Rob Lee in the dressing room."

He burst out laughing then Granville gave me another message. I relayed it, "Well, let me introduce myself. I am Bren, and delighted that I'm allowed in the press box. But I must tell you that your idea of writing a book on the five best teams of the decade is quite good and I can help you with chapter five if you want?" He went pale. "Yes I know it is a secret," I continued, "but a bit of feedback will get you through chapter five – stop worrying about it."

"How do you know?"

"As I said, I'm psychic and what's more, can I introduce you to The Pope?" pointing to Granville. "He is the ball of the stars and can tell you what's going to happen before it does. You see it's all about possibilities. I know you're still taking in what I've just told you. So when you have calmed down we will speak again." The reporter did not know what to do.

Phil, who had been listening, said, "How did you know? Is this why you have been different?"

"Yeah I suppose so. Anyway I need to do some mental exercises with the Pope before the match starts. We've only got two minutes. I'll explain everything later, okay?"

I concentrated with Granville for the next three minutes. "Well done," he said. "Once more with feeling."

I let all the noise of the balls on and off the touch-line flood in. Then I imagined Granville with a help sign stuck on him and imagined it would be quiet in two seconds and it was! "Am I getting better?" I asked.

"You sure are. The last one I didn't screen. You can do it on your own now. By the way the teams are coming out so I'll be off. If you want me you'll have to find me in the crowd of balls."

With that he was gone from my head. I concentrated on the balls on the touch-line and they all came flooding in, and somewhere out there was the Pope.

"Bren, talk to me, two heads are better than one at a game like this," interrupted Phil.

"Thirty-two," I replied.

"What?" said Phil.

"Well, if you want some help, write down whatever I say, and question it after the match – you'll be amazed." At that point the reporter who was writing the book sat next to Phil and looked across at us both in a 'Can I be in your gang?' sort of way. Most of the reporters work together in a press box. It's always possible that you can be blowing your nose when a goal goes in or watching something upfield. If you miss a detail everyone else gets then the sports editor will be on your back. As it can happen to the best of them they usually agree to help each other a bit. Then he spoke.

"Phil, do you mind me listening in? I don't know how he does it but this could be good and we'll get the edge on the other reporters – what do you think?"

Phil didn't know whether that was a compliment or not but shrugged his shoulders saying, "Okay Danny, let's do it."

We all looked out on to the pitch. The ref blew his whistle.

Phil started a running commentary.

"The Geordies have gone 4-4-2. Villa looks like three at the back with Wright pushing forward." There was a gap as the first Newcastle attack mounted. Then, "He's in space. Just play it! He was open there, the twat just didn't look up."

Danny chipped in.

"Villa just didn't close him down. If they carry on like

that they'll get slaughtered. Get a foot in!"

I watched and listened; then within thirty seconds it was a free kick from thirty yards out of the Newcastle net. The teams set up for it and I focused on the balls, and the most happiest sound of singing came through into my head...

"SOMEWHERE ---- OVER THE CROSSBAR" flooded in. I could hear Phil and Danny in the distance asking me what I thought.

"Over the crossbar," I said, "just the way Judy Garland used to sing it."

We watched and Beardsley floated it over the crossbar.

"Just like in the Wizard of Oz," I laughed.

Danny and Phil looked at me with that 'you were lucky' look. The Villa keeper, Spink, a veteran of their 1982 European Cup winning side, was about to take the goal kick and Phil and Danny started having a debate about which side Newcastle would favour as there was no obvious bias. They had Scott Sellars to offer a genuine left-sided outlet unlike a lot of teams and Beardsley had the freedom and the skill to go left if needed. I focused and all I could hear was...

"DOO DO DOO – DO – DOO DO DOO – DO – DOO DO – DO – HEY BABE WORK THE BALL ON THE WEST SIDE... DOO DO DOO..."

I switched off and said to Phil and Danny, "They'll work the west side of the stadium for a while (meaning the left side)". This later proved to be another truth, and I enjoyed the version of "Walk on the wild side".

Anyway I focused in again and worked on turning the volume down. It worked - I was getting the hang of this. I focused on one set of balls on the touch-line and they were singing; I focused on the balls in the dugouts, they were talking seriously. I focused on balls anywhere else and found the Pope talking to what seemed to be about five other balls in a very normal way, some serious talk, some joking.

"Ah hello, Bren," Granville said. "Let me introduce you to some of my old friends. Bren, please meet Stanley Matthews, Bedford Jezzard, Nobby Stiles, Peter Withe and Archie Gemmill."

"Let me introduce myself," I said and went through the 3 p's quickly.

Stanley Matthews remarked, "How long have you been training this one?"

Granville replied very proudly, "About two days – I think he could be good."

"Well I'm off for a minute or two, bye." I refocused on the touch-line balls and I wasn't even aware of what was going on with the match. From the touch-line balls I received, "CORNERFLAG PAT, CORNERFLAG PAT, HE GETS PISSED ON BY A BLACK AND WHITE CAT – EARLY IN THE MORNING..."

I looked down the pitch to see Newcastle giving away a corner. I flicked back to Granville and his mates.

"What's all this singing by the touch-line balls?"

"Oh they're young and are learning all the ball chants – but the difference between them and the spectators is that they sing about what is going to happen next rather than irrelevant songs or obscene chants."

"Thanks, bye." I chirped. I then started singing to myself "Cornerflag Pat. Cornerflag Pat."

"Bren," Phil shouted to bring me into his world, "I suppose you can talk to the corner flag now?"

"Don't be fucking stupid," I said. Phil looked hurt. "Sorry Phil. I'm with you now – what's cooking?"

"If you can pull yourself out of your reverie for a second,

did you know that ball was going for a corner?"

"Sort of." I replied.

"Well that's all well and good but it isn't the sort of insight that gets us an edge on the opposition is it?" Phil nodded in the direction of the other pressman, some of whom were giving me odd looks.

"See your point." I replied and I started to try and make contact with the balls near the dugouts. It took some effort to focus through the static but Granville exerted his influence and I found myself in communication with a ball called John Toshack. Granville explained that this was a Newcastle ball with a sense of humour that had taken the name of Keegan's former strike partner at Liverpool.

"I'm John Toshack," explained the ball, "But my friends call me Tosh."

"Good to meet you Tosh. I'm Bren, a friend of Granville Tingate. You've probably not met him have you?"

"Not before today but he introduced himself earlier. What can I do for you?"

"I'd really like to know what you heard from the Newcastle management team. Any insights?"

"Not as many as I'd like because I haven't been close enough. I was out on the pitch for the subs' warm-up during most of the team talk. I can tell you that they're worried about Howey's knee. He might have twisted it early in the game and now the bench are monitoring him to see if he has to come off."

"There's a problem with Howey," I quickly announced to Phil and Danny. "He's signalled to the bench that he's in a bit of pain."

This was more like it as far as they were concerned and they started scrutinising the Geordies' centre-half for evidence. After a minute they were doubtful but then the player signalled to the trainer and the game stopped so he could receive attention.

"Impressive," said Danny.

I went back to Tosh. "What's the word, Tosh?"

"They'll leave him on for a bit and see if he can run it off. Oh, they also want to see Beardsley dropping deeper to lose his marker – he'll play more in the 'hole'."

I passed these gems on to Danny and sure enough Beardsley was picking the ball up deeper creating problems for Villa. Defenders and midfielders couldn't work out who should be picking him up and he started to run the game. About 25 minutes in he was allowed too much time to pick out the run of midfielder Robert Lee; he controlled it expertly, holding off a despairing challenge and slotted it past Spink. It produced an explosion of noise from the Geordies and murmurs of appreciation all round the press box.

All of a sudden the discussion started. Guys shouting across the room;

"Beardsley's pass? Beardsley? Certain about that? Who missed him, Parker? That fucker never tracks back!"

Tosh told me that the goal was exactly what Keegan had hoped for. Beardsley dropping deeper to allow runners from midfield to infiltrate the box unmarked. I passed this on to Danny and Phil. To be honest things were going so well for Newcastle that there wasn't a lot more I could learn from Tosh, so I asked Granville if he had a contact in the Villa camp.

"Not really, they're all a little way off in the tunnel at the moment. We've got a fourth official who seems to be looking for things to do and he's moved them out of the way just to be tidy. They aren't pleased I can tell you. Ah, look out for this free kick."

Villa had finally made a bit of progress and Dwight Yorke took the ball with his back to goal. The left-back Beresford clattered into him and was lucky to escape with just a cautionary word from the official.

"Quick, what's going to happen?" I demanded.

"It's one small bounce for a ball and one giant swerve for ballkind," was his cryptic reply.

"Meaning what?"

"There's going to be a big swerve on the ball of course."

"Big swerve on this!" I shouted to the others.

Staunton was lining up to hit it left-footed. Phil was almost on his feet as this was one of the ex-Liverpool players. He crashed into it at pace and Srnicek in the Newcastle goal seemed to lose it for a split second; he adjusted his footing, punched it over the bar and looked ruefully at Staunton who had nearly embarrassed him with the prodigious bend he put on it. Phil began extolling his virtues.

"He didn't mean that, you know," said Tosh. "Caught it all wrong but like a good pro he's making like he intended to bend it all along."

The players started to get organised for the corner. Villa sent up their big guns from the back and the Geordie defenders started shouting to each other and pointing in that especially aimless way that convinces footballers that they're doing something useful. At that moment Nobby Stiles rolled within range of the pitch and he came into my head intoning;

"ALAS POOR GOALIE, I KNEW HIM WELL…"

"Granville, what's that about?"

"The ball's going in," he replied laconically.

"They'll score off this," I shouted.

The corner came across towards the near post straight

into a big melee of players. Srnicek came for it but couldn't get there through the crush. The ball skidded off the head of one of his own defenders and shot into the net. Jubilation on the pitch and in the Holte End. Unfortunately (for Villa) the referee had his arm up as he'd obviously spotted an infringement among all the jostling. The Villa players engaged in ritual protests but gave up when they saw Newcastle trying to take a quick one with several home players out of position.

"You need to listen to me carefully," said Granville, "I said the ball was going IN, not that Villa would score."

Back on the pitch Villa were pressing again and this time they had the ball in a dangerous spot at the right edge of the Newcastle box. Ray Houghton (ex-Liverpool) took the ball to the by-line and crossed it back, turning the defence. It hung in the air beautifully, only for two Villa strikers, Yorke and Saunders, to go for it together. Neither made a proper connection and the ball bobbled out of harm's way. The pair had a bit of a glaring session after that one and I heard Nobby's voice to the tune of Elton John;

"DON'T GO SCORING MY GOAL…"

"What's happening next then?" interrupted Danny, "What's Brian Little going to do to turn it round?"

Even though the others were catching on to the situation and my ball psychic abilities, I thought it might be a bit much to try to explain that I might find it difficult to get that information because Stanley Matthews and his mates were stuck in the tunnel. I got straight into tuning in to find a contact on the Villa bench and Nobby answered.

"I'm on the Villa bench now. Someone picked me up and I'm right by the management team so what can I tell you?"

"The guys up here want to know what Little's going to

do about the situation."

"Nothing before half-time. He thinks that the players have adjusted well enough since he passed a message to one of the midfielders to shadow Beardsley. He also thinks the ball needs to be played into feet more – the service to Saunders and Yorke's been poor."

"No changes before half-time," I told the others, and they gleefully put this straight into their reports; this gave them a head start on the rest of the pressmen who were trying to work out if Little intended to alter personnel or formation.

"And what about Newcastle?" asked Danny.

Back to Tosh again who passed on the gem that one of the subs would be warming up as a precaution because Howey seemed in pain again. I warned the lads to keep an eye on the centre-back and just on the half-time whistle he went to the touch-line for treatment.

Albert booted the ball out and it sailed right up to the press box and settled in the crowd just below us. A voice shouted, "Hi, Bren – I'm Doug Ellis (named after the notorious Villa chairman, known as 'Deadly' for his way of firing managers). How do you think I am doing? Granville told me about you – sorry we haven't been introduced."

"Fine, have a good game." I waved to the ball as started its bouncing back through the terraces. "Phil, Danny. The main ball has just said 'hello'. C'mon, wave to it!!" I demanded.

Phil and Danny looked a bit uncomfortable but nevertheless stood up, leant over the desk and waved. You should have seen the look on the other reporters' faces. It was heaven. Phil and Danny turned and enjoyed their disgusted looks.

At that point the half time whistle blew. Danny went for the grub and drinks.

"Well," said Phil, "I still don't quite believe it but I am impressed. So what is Granville like and can I speak to him?"

"Firstly, think of your ball and shout HI GRANVILLE!" Phil screwed up his face to indicate he was trying. "Well done, he heard you and hopes you have a great reporting match. Secondly, he's a bit like a guru – you know like Yoda out of the Star Wars movie, but he comes from Yorkshire originally and has travelled everywhere I think."

Phil started taking the piss by imitating Yoda in a Yorkshire voice. "Chips – some – bye – gum – have – I."

"Stop it, Phil. It's that cynicism that stops you from being able to communicate. Anyway, Granville has just told me that they are out of Bovril."

"I don't like bloody Bovril anyway. Didn't even like it when I was a kid."

"It's tradition," I countered.

"It's shite and overpriced!"

"Exactly."

Danny came barrelling back in with a tray full of food and drink, a mixture of pies, teas and Mars Bars.

"No Bovril," he explained.

"We know," both Phil and I chorused. Danny looked puzzled for a second and started handing out the goodies. The pies looked a bit suspect and turned out to be super-hot. One prick in the crust, a jet of steam filled the air and the whole thing collapsed inward. Phil and I stared and prodded around for a while but we couldn't come to a consensus on the filling. I favoured chicken and mushroom and Phil championed meat and potato.

"Vegetarian," said Danny, amused by the debate.

The refreshments were finished just as the players came back out of the tunnel. We already knew that there would be no changes on the Newcastle side because Tosh had been in the dressing room. He explained that Keegan had warned his defenders not to play too far up the park and let the Villa strikers exploit the space behind them. Danny and Phil gleefully worked this into their evolving copy. Danny surprised the rest of the pressmen by letting out a loud "Yes!" before the game had even kicked off.

Villa came out strongly as expected and the Newcastle defence were overworked for the first quarter of an hour. Srnicek dealt confidently with crosses into the box though, and for all their effort the home side didn't really produce a worthwhile opportunity. Gradually the visitors regained their ascendancy and Villa found it increasingly difficult to counter. At one point Fox reached the by-line and centred; the scramble that ensued caused great excitement in the crowd and even more mayhem in the press box.

"Who blocked the first shot?"

"Was it handball?"

"Wright, surely?"

"Ehiogu was in there as well!"

Alan Wright, Villa left-back, was one of the smallest players in the Premiership – slight, balding and white. Ugo Ehiogu, centre-back, six foot plus, heavily built and black. And the press box was divided between which of these two put in the vital challenge. Everyone was under extra pressure because the game would be televised and the hacks knew that the incident could be scrutinised by Des Lynam and the journalist's nemesis Alan Hansen. The Daily Mirror's man summed up the feeling in the box.

"For Christ's sake we've got to get it right. Fucking Captain Scarlet's going to pick that one apart with the benefit of ten different angles and slo-mo!"

"It was Wright of course," said Granville haughtily.

"There's a ball on the touch-line being held by one of the ball boys. He knew straight away it was him."

I passed this on to our pair who were relieved and jubilant as they both had doubts about the incident. After a few seconds they decided to act out of professional solidarity and set about convincing their colleagues that Wright was indeed the man, though without trying to explain why they were so certain. The herd mentality soon took over and even hacks who had been convinced that Ehiogu had thrust his left leg in there were soon deleting copy. When Match of the Day ran that night Danny and Phil would have stored away some very useful credit among their peers.

We'd only just sorted that one out when Newcastle struck again. Villa failed to deal effectively with a corner; Albert's flick-on at the near post found Cole close in on goal and he wasn't going to miss a header from three yards. The press box did a brief consultation on the flick but Granville's intervention wasn't necessary as the consensus quickly settled on Albert.

I heard Tosh say, "They just need to keep it tight from here according to McDermott." (The Geordie Assistant Manager.)

"Little's going to throw on Lamptey and try to play three up," said Nobby, adding his insight from the Villa bench.

I duly passed the information on to my friends and from then on the match lost some of its sparkle. Villa tried hard but Newcastle had things pretty much under control and towards the end they looked the more likely to score again. In the last minute Cole raced clear toward the right edge of the area and went down under a heavy challenge. The away fans bayed for a penalty, Keegan and his management team were up off the bench and everyone watched the referee.

"No way," interjected Granville. Sure enough, the official waved play on vigorously. "The replay will show that there was no contact," he added.

The lads were really keen on this bit of insight and this time they didn't feel they had to share it with their colleagues, some of whom were arguing vehemently that there was no way it couldn't have been a 'pen'. That was the last real incident and the Geordies went totally ape when the whistle blew because their team not only stayed on top of the division but played some really good stuff too. As Granville put it, Newcastle had certainly 'knocked' it.

We started clearing up in the press box. Danny turned out to be a great guy and we swapped phone numbers. Phil felt really good and invited Danny for a few pints after the report was finished. I went with Phil to his office while Danny went off to listen to the words of wisdom for his report in the Sunday Mercury. We agreed to meet at the Tavern at seven o'clock.

When we got to Phil's office, I knew I would be bored so I took Granville down to the railway sidings to meet Pongo Wareing. On the way I asked Granville why I couldn't hear all the balls before entering the stadium and he told me that balls can only project the length of a football field. He also said that with the coming of computers or more complex telephone lines, balls should be able to communicate down a phone line. He stressed he wanted to talk about it when he gave me my lessons.

We then came into range of Pongo. "I'll let you do the introductions, Bren," Granville said, then screened off.

I walked across the wasteland and there was Pongo. "Hello Pongo, how are you doing?"

"Well hello," said Pongo in a genuinely 'happy to hear

your voice' manner. "What have you been possibiliting?"

"Quite a lot this afternoon – at the match."

"Yeah I know, I wish I could have made my normal chain link of about ten balls, then I'm within range to listen to the match – but the third ball had been taken to fucking Brighton for the day."

"Well," I said proudly, "I have brought my best ballfriend to see you; let me introduce the Ball of the Stars."

Pongo interrupted. "Never, is this the amazing Granville Tingate? – I'm honoured."

"I'm very pleased to meet you and I'll give you a perfect factual replay of what you missed if you like?" said Granville.

"Excellent," said Pongo. "Any new touch-line ball chants?"

"Yes, there were a couple," said Granville. "The ball went out of the park and landed at the back of a night club owned by a guy called Sammy Franks so the touch-liners sang as it was going over, I LEFT MY BALL IN SAM FRANKS DISCO. The other was when the goalie did a high lob just missing a pigeon, to the song, YOU ARE THE BALL BENEATH MY WINGS. Well, shall we have a chat?"

I placed Granville down next to Pongo and let them get on with it. I looked back to the street and saw a local pub. So I said to Granville and Pongo, "Half an hour do, you two? I'll go and get a pint."

"Yeah, thank you," they cried in unison.

I walked off proudly thinking of what a cracking day it had been, and the three of them, Granville, Phil and Danny were happy.

I went and sat in the window of the pub so I could see them both and kept myself screened off as I was still within ball range. I let my mind drift and thought of all the things that I saw happen with the reporters in the press box. The sad thing about the guys covering the game was that most of them were too wrapped up in the demands of the job to really enjoy the spectacle. Some of them even reached the point where every incident seemed to add to the pressure. They gave the distinct impression that a dour, colourless 0-0 draw would be right up their street.

And there was pressure. We hung around for a while to listen to the blokes who were phoning copy in for the evening sports papers and then they were dashing off to the press conferences to compose yet more immediate copy for later editions and back pages. No one wanted to miss a quote and they were all busy trying to sift the information and stitch it into pithy phrases with deadlines hanging over them. I began to wonder whether I really did fancy the idea of doing this for a living. That is, unless I could have Granville in the box all the time.

Then, I don't know why, I thought of Catrina. Why? They weren't nasty thoughts or pleasant thoughts, they were just aimless driftings about anything, but she would be there. At the time I thought it was strange.

I went to pick up Granville and asked Pongo sincerely if he wanted to come with us. He gave me a philosophical reply.

"I live the true art of Zen balls. I am on the watercourse way; I will continue to bob up and down around here for a while and who knows, our paths may cross again – the odds are good. By the way the odds bit wasn't Zen. Thank you and bye for now."

We went off to get Phil. Danny had completed his match report and was bubbling. We walked in and straight away

Phil said smugly that we were off for some beers then a take-away back to his place. Danny would be coming back too so we could have a game of trivia or something.

"I hate trivia," I moaned.

"Well, anything you like then," said Phil genuinely trying to please.

Granville threw me a quick one. I threw the gauntlet down to Phil and Danny. "Okay, we get a few extra beers to loosen the brain cells, then we play FOOTBALL MONOPOLY. Me and Granville against you and Danny. I'll explain the rules later. You have still got your monopoly board haven't you, Phil?"

"Yeah, sounds GERRRATE."

So that was decided. It was off to the pub with Granville well screened so no more fighting started, and then a carry-out to give us energy for the big game.

Chapter 4 – The Big Monopoly Game

Two hours later we were sitting round the kitchen table with Phil and Danny. The table had been cleared and Granville sat opposite me. The monopoly board and its bits were laid on the table with a large litre bottle of vodka and two cartons of orange juice. Phil had made his kitchen sparse but comfortable. All the instruments for a good Italian were hung neatly on the wall with everything else in its place. His table was the best thing – oblong and big enough for six to sit round. It was an old butcher's table and had all the indents, or as Phil would say, it had been distressed. I thought of all the animals that would have been hacked up into pieces and thought yeah, the animals would have been fucking distressed.

I had put the monopoly board out on the table whilst Phil and Danny were wandering round talking shop. I'd poured them a drink – triple vodka and orange – and followed them into the other room; then I carefully pinched a cushion and took Granville through to the kitchen, placing him on a chair supported by a stack of cookery books and the cushion.

Granville said, "I hope you know that I am indulging you on this game because you took me to the match and introduced me to Pongo. Our real mission starts tomorrow when Phil goes out to meet his new girlfriend."

"New girlfriend," I cried. "What about Catty?"

"Well I'm pissed off now," exclaimed Granville. "Your answer should have been – what's our mission? Mind you,

you have been thinking about her more than you would concede. She is a good choice as she's a ball psychic too, you know – she just hasn't tried it yet. Possibly more importantly she could blossom with the right person, and that could be you if you care to take your head out from up your arse to think about it."

"Don't go heavy on me. I've had a good day up to now."

"Good day!" screamed Granville, "It's been the most illuminating and amazing day you have ever had – anyway tomorrow we begin."

"Okay. Sorry for being an arsehole."

"Accepted," stated Granville in his most fatherly voice.

"Can I interrupt?" said Danny as he crept through sheepishly. "I assume you were doing your psychic thing with the ball, sorry, the Pope; but I wonder if we could start, and anyway, how do we play football monopoly?"

"Sorry, Danny. I'll explain and if I am slightly wrong Granville will chip in and correct me."

Phil smirked and said, "I don't believe I'm doing this, playing with a football. But seeing as we are having a great day and I am completely pissed, let's go. Give us the rules, Bren."

It took me a few minutes because you know what it's like when you're trying to explain something factual that has procedures to a couple of people who are pissed. They constantly say things like, 'Oh yeah, got it,' then proceed to double check by saying 'So if…' and get it completely wrong.

Anyway I explained the rules. Quite simple they are too. Things like jail and community chest remain the same, but the basics are different. The aim is to make as much monopoly money as possible, and possibly secure as much real money for five years time.

Every player throws the dice in turn and as we were teams of two, either one or both could offer solutions. When you land on something e.g. Coventry Street, which is yellow, you can offer the following:

1   any sports team or individual colour or name connection (not football) gets you £20 and to stay without fines
2   any football team colour connection gets you £50 from the bank
3   any team/player connection to the square name gets you £100 from the bank
4   you have £1000 to start with

If you can't offer a connection then you have to pay a £250 fine to the opposite team (all square cards are shuffled at the beginning and divided up). So as you keep going round, you run out of connections.

Now, that's the monopoly money bit. Granville's possibilities bit is very simple. Whilst discussion takes place about teams and players etc, you can try and predict what will be happening with that team or player in exactly five years from now. Everyone has a pen and paper with an envelope. Quite simply you say something like 'Keegan will be prime minister', put it on paper and state what you will pay if it does not occur (e.g. a quid) and then write it down. Let the others write it down and at the end everyone signs. We each sign each other's sheet and seal the envelope with the exact date for it to be opened in five years.

By the way if you do this on a regular basis with friends, say once a month, you could make some money if you have thought things through.

"Anyway," I screamed, "let battle commence". I passed

the dice to Phil who was still staring at Granville a bit dubiously. He took it and threw a one, which put him on Old Kent Road. Danny and Phil looked at each other a bit and then Danny chipped in cautiously.

"Gillingham are the only current league club in Kent."

"There you go," I said encouragingly. "That gets you £100."

I took charge of the dice, certain in the knowledge that Granville was unlikely to object. It was something of an anti-climax to throw a two and land on Community Chest. We got a Get Out of Jail card but I was itching to get into it and listen to Granville in action. Phil looked like he wanted to join in now and quickly threw a five that put them on The Angel, Islington.

"Brett Angell. Big striker at Everton." He thought for a second. "At Stockport as well," he added with a flourish.

He got a pat on the back from Danny and downed a wacking swig of vodka in triumph. I remembered just how competitive he is. It was all the more galling to then get a two and land on Income Tax. Minus £200 already and still no questions answered. Danny stretched for the dice and sent it spinning off the board to the corner of the room; it lodged on six, which placed their car on the Electric Company and that proved a bit more of a tester for the journos. After a few minutes the best they could come up with was NORWEB sponsoring Wigan in their RL glory days. I wanted to smile a bit but held it back. Granville tuned in and said we wouldn't have a problem on that square.

Their turn again and four took them to Bow Street. Danny went straight for Dundee United's club colours. Only £50 though and Granville explained that they'd be struggling if they had to find more teams in orange. At the moment though, Phil seemed cocky. Mind you, this was partly because he still believed they were only really playing me. Where my insights at the match came from he didn't know, but he still couldn't get his head round the concept of a psychic ball. Or a ball psychic.

I launched the dice for a five and moved the boot to Pentonville. Granville passed me some speedy information.

"George Best was sent to Pentonville for drink driving. He was there on Christmas Day 1984." I looked confident as I relayed the information; now we were in the game and the opposition was impressed. My turn for vodka.

"Don't drink it!" said Granville with great authority. "Ask Phil if he has still got some white rum from Mauritius?" I looked at Phil whilst my head was cocked towards Granville.

"Have you still got that bottle of white rum?"

Phil answered, "Yeah, it's in the top cupboard on the right – wait a minute, how did you know?"

"Granville has just told me. By the way do you still have coconut milk and that carton of fresh pineapple juice?"

"Yeah, it's in the fridge," he answered whilst shaking his head at me. Then he started his comfort behaviour of running his fingers through his hair.

"Want some hair gel?" I smirked and proceeded to help myself to the ingredients – one sixth coconut milk, then fill to one third rum, then top up with juice and a couple of ice cubes.

"That looks disgusting!" said Phil trying not to touch his hair.

"Have a taste." I offered it to them both. They had a sip and both said that they had found heaven.

"That," I said, "is a real Pina Colada!"

Phil laughed and said, "I didn't know you were into

cocktails?"

"I'm not. Granville told me the mix. Mmm tastes good, and by golly it does you good." I tried to remember where I had heard the by golly bit – somewhere on a television advert from years ago, I think.

"Not too much," cautioned Granville.

"We need to have a prediction here," I suggested (probably the association of George Best and vodka). "What will George Best be doing in the year 2000?"

It took a little time for the three of us to write down the predictions. I just put down the words from Granville, then we passed them round to read. Phil's said he thought the guy would be running a night-club somewhere. Danny was (I thought) wildly optimistic, stating that he thought George would be in soccer management. Granville was blunt – he thought George would be in hospital. Remembering the Wogan Show this seemed all too realistic.

Next throw Phil produced a three, which put them on Vine Street, another orange square. They ummed and ahhed for a bit but had to fall back on Blackpool's tangerine colours.

"They're running out of options already," said Granville.

We got a three as well, which put us on the Electric Company. Granville was true to his word and sent in a cracking answer. I made a show of thinking it over and gave them the hope that we were having as much trouble as they had on the same spot. Rubbing my chin added to the effect, until I feigned inspiration.

"Ever Ready are one of the top sides in the Bolivian League."

"Fucking hell!" said Danny shaking his head.

"Bastard!" added Phil.

I took this to mean that they had at least heard of Ever

Ready. I raised my glass to them. Danny grinned, Phil swore again and Granville told me to watch the drinking. I assured him that I had every intention of staying at least aware of events. If Granville carried on like this I'd have to limit the celebratory swigs to one every ten answers.

I had to let go, so I picked up Granville and jumped to the kitchen door within sight of Phil's entrance hall. I gave Granville such a boot down the hallway that he rattled off the coat hangers, brollies and assorted footwear and left the end of the hallway like a scene from a war zone.

"Thanks, Bren," said Granville as I placed him back on the cushion.

Danny laughed with great gusto and said, "I hope you're not going to do that to me, Phil, if I give a good answer?"

"Let's get on with the game," Phil said, as he shrugged his shoulders and sank into the table, using his glass to prop himself up. Granville and I were getting to him, I thought.

And carry on like that it did.

Phil and Danny threw three – hit Community Chest and got a Drunk in Charge card.

Granville and I threw three to land on Marylebone Station. I chipped in before Granville with MCC.

I'll abbreviate the names from here so you can get the answers we came up with.

P&D – hit a five to Coventry Street. Answer Coventry City won the FA Cup for the only time in 1987.

G&B – threw a one to Vine Street. Answer Holland 1974 World Cup Final playing in orange- Granville reckons that is the end of the orange colours.

P&D – landed on Waterworks. Danny has an inspiration and says River Plate, top club in Argentina.

G&B – threw one, hit Community Chest and drew Advance to Go card.

P&D – six to go to Bond Street. Answer John Bond manager of Man City in 1981 Cup Final – follow that with four, hit Super Tax and lose £100.

G&B – two, another visit to Community Chest and pay doctor's fee £50.

P&D – five took them to Whitechapel. Struggle at first but split the name and go for John White, inside-forward in Spurs Double team in 1961, tragically killed in 1964 on a golf course.

G&B – four to land on Angel. Phil argued that the blue colour is sky blue not dark blue so I couldn't have Chelsea. Granville said take Man City colour then.

P&D – they also land on Angel. Immediately chose Coventry, also sky blue.

G&B – threw two. Landed on Euston. To stop Phil being cocky we answered that Chelsea had light blue in their original colours thus getting them in after all. Phil insisted on checking this but it is true, as they were the racing colours of the Earl of Cadogan, the first club President.

P&D – five took them to Pall Mall. Debate about what colour these squares are. I thought pink. Phil said mauve but admits to being colour-blind. I relented and Danny chipped in Anderlecht, Belgium's greatest club, who play in mauve and white.

G&B – landed them on the dreaded Electric Co again. Granville stepped in easily though with the first floodlit league match in 1956, Portsmouth v. Newcastle

P&D – four to land on Marylebone station – they can't answer and get £250 fine.

G&B – one, Whitehall. As P&D split the word 'Whitechapel', I split 'WhiteHall', and offered either the fact that the white ball only became standard in 1951 or the 'White Horse FA Cup Final' in 1923.

P&D – Free Parking – toilet break.

At this point Danny leant over and said, "Remember earlier when you were telling me about the Pope's unusual view on life – what were the three P's again?"

Danny had really caught me out as I was in no position to talk philosophy – football yes but not philosophy. I responded off the top of my head. "Pelicans, Pox and Plankton."

"No, that can't be right. The last one was Possibilities wasn't it?"

I thought, 'I'm not going to get out of this' and suggested that he try and talk to Granville himself. Danny turned to Granville and stared and concentrated. His face went as red as a beetroot and his muscles tensed in his face so he looked like a bag of spanners – he lasted about a minute then broke wind loudly. Danny jumped up out of his stupor just as Phil walked back into the kitchen.

"My God!" said Phil with that brilliant look of 'I don't do those sort of things', "Danny, go for a shit quickly!"

Danny was embarrassed – very embarrassed. Phil nipped into the other room for some air freshener and Granville spoke quickly. "He's got possibilities of being ball psychic, because I heard a faint 'hello I'm Danny'. By the way I knew he was going to fart loudly; it was an inevitable possibility!"

I told Danny and stroked his arm, giving him the biggest buzz of the night – he had made contact.

Phil walked back through to observe me stroking Danny and shouted, "That's enough!"

Danny and I laughed. I realised I had just made someone very happy and had made a special kind of friend. I told Phil to 'Fuck off!' and carried on with the game…

G&B – landed on the orange set again; Bow Street. I

scratched my head while Granville tried to get me to realise how easy it was. "Think of me with a suntan." I realised he meant the orange ball used in snowy weather.

P&D – come out of FP on to Fleet Street – take the easy option of Man Utd in red.

G&B – six to Chance, receive £150 from building soc.

G&B – six to the Waterworks – answer Goole Town's water tower vantage point.

G&B – one to Piccadilly – answer Norwich City play in yellow.

Danny called for another prediction here. His challenge was where would Norwich be in 2000? The previous season they had played in the UEFA cup and beaten Bayern Munich. At the time this match was played, they were 6th in the Premier, but they ended up relegated at the end of the season and have been in Div 1 since.

Phil said, "They are a solid team who can 'knock' it. I predict they will stay in Premier and might win a cup or two."

Danny seemed more pessimistic – he thought that it would go wrong, and they'd sink to Div 2 and be forced to sell players.

Granville tended to agree with this prediction and I went along with him. Phil of course vehemently disagreed.

Then we got on with the game.

P&D – one to Trafalgar. Made the connection to Nelson and go for Garry Nelson, journeyman forward with Charlton and several other clubs. I thought that the Nelson connection was a bit dubious but Granville says accept it because he can top it later.

G&B – three to Oxford Street. Answer Oxford United only joined Football League in 1962.

P&D – two to Leicester Square, went for Leicester City

losing 4 times in FA Cup Finals at Wembley – three in the 60's.

G&B – six to land on Super Tax.

G&B – five to Whitechapel, Granville throws in a peach. The 'White Arrow', nickname of the legendary Alfredo Di Stefano.

P&D – to Community Chest – picked up a fine.

G&B – two to Kings Cross – Granville mentioned George V as first monarch to go to an FA Cup Final in 1914.

P&D – six to Bond Street. Answer Plymouth Argyle as only league club with green as first choice strip.

P&D – six took them to Go.

P&D – five to Kings Cross. Answer Cross Keys, Welsh RU team.

G&B – five, Just Visiting.

P&D – a five, also Just Visiting.

G&B – a two to go on the Electric Co. again. Danny and Phil thought this would catch G&B out but Granville smoothly passed on an answer about the first use of undersoil heating – at Everton in 1958.

P&D – threw six. Placed them on Bow Street – the difficult orange colour. Couldn't produce anything so were fined £250 again and forfeited their extra go because they failed to answer.

G&B – threw four and also ended up on Bow Street. Granville pulled off a masterstroke by using the name of Floyd Streete, former Wolves defender. This really upset Phil and Danny who were really beginning to see the writing on the wall.

P&D - five to the Strand. Answer Swindon Town play in red.

G&B – one to chance and win £100.

P&D – also to chance – win £50.

G&B – Free Parking – time for food break.

P&D – moved on to Trafalgar – this time they answered Bristol City play in red.

G&B – also landed on Trafalgar. Granville played them at the Nelson game by answering the team Nelson who were members of the Football League 1921-31.

P&D – three to Coventry Street. Answered Coventry Bees speedway team.

G&B – two, Leicester Square. Answered Arsenal's original name was 'Dial Square'. Well, the kitchen erupted.

"This is fucking ridiculous!" exclaimed Phil. "You can't have it just because you landed on a square shape."

Danny joined in and looked at Granville. "I wouldn't have thought you would have stooped that low – you being the Pope and all that. I expected better of you."

"Wait a minute." I called time. "What made you think it was Granville's answer. Do you think I've been sat here all night taking advice from him? C'mon guys, give me some credit. You have started to address Granville only with your comments and I'm in this fucking game as well!"

I picked up Granville and opened the kitchen window. A good well-aimed drop kick sent him arching over the back garden to land in the branches of the tree. Granville then rattled down through the tree to land on the grass. At that point the mysterious little head popped over the fence with the little white knuckles clinging on. "And you can fuck off as well!" I shouted. The head disappeared like a rocket.

"Calm down. Calm down, Bren." Danny came across and patted my back. I started to cool off and paced the kitchen for a couple of minutes whilst Phil and Danny talked quietly of how many answers came from me and how many came from Granville. I must admit they gave me credit for more than I really answered. I started feeling better.

I looked out to Granville and no response! Shit, I thought. Oh dear I have really upset him now.

I turned to Phil and Danny and said, "Looks like the game is off – the Pope has fucked off!"

We carried on talking for a while. Then Danny wanted us all to check our winnings. We were £1170 in credit and Phil and Danny were down to their last £130. Danny said we had to carry on and Phil eventually agreed. I walked across to the window with my drink in my hand and leant out.

"Well, are we going to finish this game or not?" Granville said in a happy tone of voice.

"Sure," I replied, "I'll come and get you – and sorry for being an arsehole."

"You being an arsehole was always a possibility. I switched off because I was talking to someone about a personal issue."

We all got settled and got some crisps and biscuits out whilst Danny bounced Granville on the kitchen floor. We carried on…

P&D – four to Regent St. Answer Celtic play in green and white.

G&B – five also to Regent Street. Answer St Etienne the famous French team known as 'les Verts'.

P&D – six to Park Lane. Opt for Queens Park Rangers.

P&D – two to Mayfair. Answer Scotland play in dark blue.

G&B – four to Liverpool Street Station. Granville showed off a bit by going for Forfar Athletic who play at Station Park.

P&D – two, Old Kent Road. Answer Maidstone, a Kent Team who used to be in the F. League.

G&B – two to Park Lane. Went for 'Bronco' Lane, one of the Sheffield Wednesday players caught in the 1965 bribery scandal.

P&D – five, Angel Islington. After difficulty came up with Argentina (light blue stripes).

G&B – got a five onto Community Chest. It said advance to Marylebone, possibly a problem but Granville had the answer – football used to be one of several sports played at Lord's, the home of MCC, in its early days.

P&D – one, landed on Chance and had to pay school fees – beginning to get annoyed?

G&B – six took them to Strand. Opted for red shirts worn by England 1966 World Cup side.

G&B – six to Coventry Street. Answer Coventry City were originally called Singers F.C. works team.

G&B – one, Waterworks. Answer Middlesborough are set to move to the Riverside Stadium.

This time Phil was getting into the prediction lark and challenged us to say who would be managing England at the millennium. He had no doubts, and asserted that Venables would still be there after winning Euro 96. Danny didn't go along with that and thought that Kevin Keegan would be in place by then. Granville actually agreed with this statement but I didn't. I thought he couldn't be right at everything, and I said Glen Hoddle would be the boss in 2000. I should have listened to him!

Back to the game.

Phil – Venables to still be there after winning Euro 96.

Danny – Kevin Keegan.

G/B – Granville thinks KEEGAN but Bren favours Glenn Hoddle.

P&D – three, Just Visiting.

G&B – three to Regent Street. Answer Hibs play in

green shirts.

P&D – fined again Marylebone?

G&B – six to Park Lane. Chelsea play in dark blue and I was getting cocky and to wind Phil up I passed up the choice of an extra go.

P&D – six to Free Parking.

P&D – two to Chance. Told to advance to Mayfair. Answer Dundee play in dark blue.

G&B – four, copped for Income Tax £200.

P&D – five, also got Income Tax.

G&B – six, Just Visiting.

G&B – four, Northumberland Avenue. Answer the reason Tottenham are called Hotspur is that the Earl of Northumberland owned a great deal of property in the area. Hotspur was his famous heroic ancestor immortalised by Shakespeare.

P&D – four to Euston. Answer Cambridge are the Light blues in the Boat Race.

G&B – three to Community Chest. £50 for 2nd in Beauty contest. At this point Granville started on the concept of beauty. I told him to leave it until the morning. Danny chipped in with something about he had had his hair cut today. Something is filtering through, I thought. Danny could maybe make the grade after all?

P&D – five, Whitehall. Answer Brian Hall member of Liverpool Cup final team in 1971. Unusual because he had a degree.

G&B – one, Marlborough. Answer Marlborough School were represented in the early meetings to codify the rules of the game around the 1860s.

It was at this point that we totted up the winnings and noted that Phil and Danny were in some real trouble.

P&D – threw six to Vine and had to come up with an

orange to stay in the game. Somehow Danny or Phil came up with South African side Kaizer Chiefs who play in that colour.

P&D – two took them to Strand. Easy answer Liverpool play in red.

G&B – four to chance. Got a Speeding Fine.

P&D – three to Trafalgar. Go for Rotherham playing in red.

G&B – five to Coventry Street. Answer that before changing to Sky Blues the team were the Bantams.

P&D – four to Waterworks. Couldn't answer – down to £10. They could have answered if they thought of other sports but they're demoralised by now.

G&B – four, Go to Jail. Played their get out card.

P&D – four to Oxford Street. Crap answer – Oxford are in the Boat Race.

G&B – four, Northumberland Ave. again. Answer Walthamstow Avenue, famous non-league side twice finalists in the old F.A Amateur Cup.

P&D – five to Park Lane. Answer Oxford are the dark blues in the Boat Race – they were really struggling now.

G&B – three to Community Chest Go to Old Kent Road. Answer Gillingham's former name was New Brompton.

P&D – four to Community Chest pay £100 wiped them out.

GAME OVER

The only square not landed on was Fenchurch St Station.

Chapter 5 – Lesson One

We all woke up the next morning and did not talk for a while. We just staggered around slowly, smiling and rubbing our heads whilst looking for our relative socks and pants, examining them to see if they were really ours. Danny broke the silence.

"Fucking amazing night, eh?"

"Yeah," I said three times really slowly. Phil started to twitch in his face. I thought, what's he up to now. I knew when he had something going for himself and was about to break the news.

"Bren, I've got to go out for a while – it's personal, you know," Phil said in his calmest of voices.

"Is she shallow?" I muttered.

"How did you know?"

"Just flicked through the possibilities as you were talking. What do I say to Catrina if she rings?" I asked knowingly.

"Tell her I will be incredibly busy for the next few weeks and will be going somewhere away from here with work and can't be contacted," Phil replied with a 'help me mate' kind of look.

"Okay," I said. At that point Danny knew he was listening to something he wasn't involved with and jumped up.

"Look at the time." He put on a good show. "I'd better be off. Thanks for a brilliant night. Nice meeting you, Bren – you've got a real future in sports writing. If you ever need a contact, give me a ring." He looked at Granville. "Thanks for everything."

"I'll tell him later," I said in a matter of fact tone. "He's talking to a ball in the street at the moment and I don't want to interrupt them as it's personal – you know, ball things."

"Okay. I'm gone," said Danny and eased his way across the floor in a delicate manner. I thought, it'll take him a while to come round from last night.

Danny left and I looked round to see Phil with his wallet in his hand. He was ready to go as well.

"Do you want to talk about it?" I asked.

"No, not really. It's been going on for a while and then it all happened this last week and I think I'm more in love than I have ever been."

"Okay," I said. "Good luck. When will I see you because I'm booked on the five o'clock train this afternoon?"

"If I'm not back, leave the key under the plant pot outside and I'll give you a ring. I don't think I could cope with another day with you and Granville anyway, even though if what's happening is real I should stay. I'm off."

With that Phil left clutching his wallet. I felt down as I had hoped we could continue the roller-coaster ride of the events together. The day took a more serious turn.

I made some coffee and Granville linked up.

"Okay, my friend. Are you ready for your first lesson?"

"Yeah, but take it steady with my head," I asked, to be treated gently.

"We'll go at your speed and link to whatever comes into your brain naturally. I don't believe in having set agendas. We will start with where you are or, as we say in the trade, kick from where you're at!!"

"I'm sorry," I said. "I still feel a little bit angry at Phil – you know, about Catty."

"Don't worry, she'll be calling later and we'll deal with it together. As for your anger, do you know how anger works and where its roots are in your brain?"

"No. In fact I'm not normally an angry person. Anyway how does this link to football?"

"It's not just football you are having lessons in, it's also life… but as I said, we will kick from where you're at and we'll start with the history of football from a psychophysiological aspect, with the focus on anger."

"You're going to be heavy, aren't you? Is this because of last night – the anger bit?"

"No, not at all. You start and I will fill in the gaps."

I fumbled to start with and started off talking about how the first type of football was probably soldiers kicking a severed head around in ancient times, then you get various soccer-like games recorded in different parts of the world, sometimes as fun and also on occasions deadly serious. The Mayans had a form of team ball game that went on for up to two days on an enclosed court and unfortunately the penalty for losing was severe; the losers were executed. Plenty to get angry about if you lasted that long, eh?

"Mm," Granville replied. "The women out there, in particular the Amara and Quechua Indians who are descendants of the Mayans, were great in anger management. They did it all with their dresses you know. It's an accepted study nowadays that men always look at a woman's behind for distraction and pleasure. Yet if you asked most males world-wide, they don't know why they look at womens behinds."

'Nice arse' came into my mind and I tittered.

"Well, they all wear layers of petticoats to exaggerate their behinds because the reason for the attraction to look there from males is not for anal sex – it's for child bearing qualities. Nice round broad hips is what the male looks at, and it goes down to the very primeval soul.

"Also in respect of what females look at, it's the male behind. To see if it is small and round which denotes fitness. Then the women can choose a fit partner who is likely to be able to hunt and protect. Hence women always commenting on footballers' small cute behinds. I always listen to females when watching a match in regard to players, fitness, i.e. if their behind is tight and cute on the day, they most likely are match fit!"

This threw me a little but I carried on.

"The Chinese played a game called Tsu Chu as far back as 206 BC; it was a bit like some of the games kids play in playgrounds with two teams trying to shoot a ball through a hole. It is recorded that the winners were rewarded with silver cups of wine and the losers received 'vigorous chastisement'."

Granville laughed. "Did you know that Chinese women prolong sexual intercourse by inserting a string of beads into a male's rectum. This puts pressure on the prostrate glands and stops the man ejaculating, and when the woman is satisfied she can pull the beads out slowly to give the world's best orgasm for the man."

I laughed out loud and said, "I have pictures now of players running round with a set of team-coloured beads up their arses and when they score they shove their hands down their shorts and prolong the ecstasy."

"Good. You're thinking well now. Myself and other balls have suggested this to a couple of ball psychic managers but did not get a big response. Alex Ferguson was one of them but he didn't take kindly to the suggestion. We tried it out on Barry Fry because he seemed like the sort of bloke who'd try anything once, but to be honest he had wilder ideas then we had."

I continued the history lesson.

"The Romans had a game called Harpastum, the Greeks played Episkyros, and the Japanese enjoyed themselves playing Kemari. By 1000 the Normans had a game called Le Soule, which they brought to England after the Conquest. Mind you, the English had been playing before then. According to one Roman historian there was a big game in 217 when a British team defeated the Roman garrison."

"The first recognisable team games appear around the twelfth century and were characterised by extreme violence and anarchy. These were huge games of up to 200 a side sometimes, which usually ended up in big communal fights. Gradually (by 1560ish) these games tended to take place on Shrove Tuesday (no need for a fixture computer). The writer Philip Stubbes described these matches (and here I cleared my throat self-importantly) 'And sometime fighting, brawling, contention, general picking, murder, homicide, and great effusion of blood, as experience daily teacheth'.

"I read that in a book somewhere and it seemed appropriate after I got caught up in a riot at a game," I explained.

"Let me explain something to you," interjected Granville, "you remember when we went to the match and you caused all that trouble in the pub, and I said it was your hypathalamus. Well it works like this: below your main part of the brain there is the hypathalamus and the best way to think of it is a room with three people in. Firstly, a sex-crazed monkey who can only think of the basics in life like sex, warmth, food etc. Secondly a pure virgin nun who has a very high moral standing and lastly a timid bank clerk who is refereeing the other two. Every thing that you think or do or receive through your senses goes through this room in a fraction of a second and therefore, it depends upon who is winning at the moment. For example if you are walking down a street thinking of buying a paper and pass a good-looking woman then all thoughts will be diverted by the mad monkey. If your nun happens to be winning, that's when you mutter comments to yourself about the ridiculously short skirt and she should be ashamed. If the bank clerk is winning then you don't know what to think and start acting and thinking about things you have to organise and do, because this gives you something simple to hinge on. After the girl passes you pat yourself on the back at not allowing yourself or your thoughts to get involved.

"So, in terms of football being violent in the early days, this is the reason as not many people had moral instruction hence the monkey having full play in a match."

"So is that why footballers had to become professional?" I said. "Because of the influence of education, i.e. the nun wanting to be on the pitch? And these matches still take place today though people don't get killed."

"Yeah, the very first professional footballers were in the fifteenth century when the Prior of Bicester paid footballers to play on Saints days and holidays."

Granville continued, "Up to 1863 you couldn't really distinguish football from rugby. You could still handle it and passing forward wasn't allowed; it was legitimate to hack at an opponent's shins to bring him down."

"What changed things was the gradual development of variations of football in the great public schools – Eton, Harrow, Winchester and Rugby all had their own variations and in the Victorian age it became thought of as manly and Christian to take part in athletic, team sports; in effect to tame the monkey. The Harrow game came closest to what we now see – they had eleven a side, throw-ins, goal-kicks and offside, while at Rugby they were still basically smashing hell out of each other and at Eton they were shoving each other and the ball up and down a wall. Winchester on the other hand had a game that completely banned handling, basically because they had less space to play in.

"With their Victorian competitive spirit, these gentlemen wanted to play each other but it was difficult without a code of rules. So in October 1863 a number of delegates met to draw up the rules of Association Football. There was a big argument about handling being banned and Blackheath withdrew because the rules banned hacking. The rest of the clubs (either public schools or teams formed by ex-schoolboys) agreed on the basics, although they still kept playing other versions in other parts of the country (Uppingham for instance – 15 a side and a huge goal). The teams present that day called themselves the Football Association.

"In 1871, the FA decided to have a cup competition to encourage the spread of their game and you could argue that this succeeded quite well. Only 15 teams were in the first cup but soon after it caught on."

"Can we have a break while I make myself some coffee and sandwiches?" I asked.

"Okay," said Granville. "Catty will be ringing in a couple of minutes."

I mooched around the kitchen thinking of what had been said. Then, as I walked back into the room, the phone rang.

"Right, Bren," Granville said with urgency, "pick up the phone and put it next to me as close as you can get. You'll hear her through me and she will hear you through me. Quick – DO IT!"

I did what I was told and held the phone next to Granville on the window sill. I heard Catrina's voice clearly. In fact it was clearer than the normal reception.

"Hi, it's Catrina!"

I answered whilst still stood up and must have been a good three feet away from the mouthpiece. "Hi, it's Bren. Phil's not here at the moment."

"Your voice is faint; can you speak up?" she replied.

"It's a bad line but think of Phil's room and the ball on the window sill and I'm sure it will be clearer." I was making it up as I was going along.

"Good," whispered Granville.

"Can you hear me now?" I asked.

"Yes. That's much better. Where is Phil?"

"I must speak to you about this, and it would be best if you listened to everything I am about to say. I know you have strong feelings for Phil and you are expecting him to be here as you arranged, and you are possibly wondering what this is about. Well, I am a little upset that I have to give you some news and…"

I couldn't believe it. Granville was talking directly to Catty and she was answering as though it was me! Granville told me later that all balls imitate; Granville's Yorkshire voice was one he had chosen and therefore it was simple for him to imitate my voice. He did however add that it was one of the ball rules never to imitate human psychic unless it was absolutely important. Well, he proceeded to have a conversation for fifteen minutes and did not let Phil down but somehow made it clear that she would need to occupy herself and not rely on Phil continuing the relationship when he returned from his fictitious trip away. I was impressed. I looked up out of the window and there was that young boy hanging and vibrating on the garden fence, looking at me holding the phone next to Granville. I lifted the phone up and interrupted. The boy's head shot out of sight.

"Well, Catty, I'd best be off now – nice speaking to you."

"Bren," she said, as though she did not want me to go. "Thanks for what you just said. I didn't think things would work out completely with Phil and me. But you have given me faith that there are some men – no I'll correct that – there is a man with honesty and sensitivity out there. I must go. Thanks Bren. If I ever meet up with you, I owe you one. Bye."

I was a bit shell-shocked myself.

Granville came into my head in a soothing manner.

"Bren, you can assimilate all this later; we need time to continue."

"Okay." I sat down. "What's next?"

"It's up to you where we start." he said.

"Okay, what about other ball psychics? Who are they? And when did you meet them?"

"Well, I've met a few. But let me tell you that they are few and far between. I suppose it's a bit like people who have rare blood groups. You are good, Bren, but like most skills and talents, it's how you use them that counts. Anyway let me see, I'll talk about ball psychics that you possibly know. For a start let's look at football commentators. You know Jimmy Greaves of the programme Saint and Greavesy – well, Jimmy was good and you must have noticed that sometimes he wasn't quite with the Saint. He was normally talking to the balls in the dugout but obviously couldn't tell ten million viewers what he was doing so he would use his get out clause, 'It's a funny old game'.

"David Coleman was definitely ball psychic. Remember the definitive way he used to shout 'one-nil'? That's because he was always certain it was going in and he knew it wasn't going to be disallowed."

"Also, referees are quite intriguing. There are one or two who can link up, but they usually crack up after a few seasons. Have you ever noticed that sometimes a ref picks up the ball and almost throttles it underneath his arm at the start of the game? He's most likely talking to the ball, saying something like 'Are you the clever shit that I had last time I was in this park? Well don't interrupt my decision-making this week'. Also sometimes when they run off to the touch-line they aren't going to talk to the linesman, they are talking to the dugout balls. They usually have to get a bit nearer to link because the touch-line balls are singing their ball chants too loud.

"Sometimes it can go to their heads though. Years ago there was a ref in Colombia who found out he was ball psychic and he started acting a bit strange. It all culminated in him sending Pele off in an exhibition game – he only just got out of that ground alive, because most of the spectators had spent what was a fortune for them to watch the greatest player ever in action. Eventually he was 'persuaded' to change his decision."

"Okay." I stood up and called time-out. "I need a cuppa. By the way, while I'm making the tea, how did you do the business with Catrina?"

"Simple," said Granville. "I used the NATO and World Health Council negotiating model. All I wanted in effect was to negotiate the fact that Phil is otherwise occupied and she has to move on. The model is simple. There are nine stages:

– Acknowledge their feelings.

- Acknowledge their truths.
- Acknowledge where they are probably right.

"That's the first three that start with acknowledging the person you are talking to. As I spoke to Catty I started with her feelings about being upset that Phil wasn't there, moved on to what she saw as being true and then went into the next three stages straightaway, which are:

- State your feelings.
- State your wants.
- State the options.

"So I showed her I am human and that I have feelings about the situation, said what I wanted and then offered her options of what she wanted to do. You see, after stroking her three times you can then show your feelings and bring in quickly what you want, but then immediately give her some options. The last three are easy:

- Commitment to discuss it.
- Clarify the issues.
- Communicate like two adults.

"So commitment is to move on. If they argue or become negative at this point – go back to the beginning. If they agree to talk a bit more then clarify the issues and chew the fat. Lastly keep up the dialogue and don't drop into childlike or mothering parent mode and you will always have a positive outcome."

"Wow!" I was impressed. "I can see how you did it – this is a pretty powerful tool."

"Yes, and it helps you keep on the straight and narrow of adult communication. Some people can focus well but forget they are humans and need to get the feelings part sorted as well. Remember, just think AAASSSCCC or ASC – I got this from staying with a top psychologist whose main role was conflict negotiation. What finished it well with

Catty was that even though you interrupted, you did not ask for anything in return for your hard work. You said goodbye simply and politely which stroked her even more, hence her parting words to you. Practice it and live it. Your returns will be tenfold."

"It's a bit too much to think about whilst you're doing it."

"Practice makes perfect," Granville replied. "This is a conscious model. Therefore you can plan ahead in most situations."

It was three o'clock by now and my head was starting to throb.

"I'll have to go soon, so can we have the last hour on something a little lighter?"

"Sure, do you want a few inside ball facts and stories?"

"Yeah," I replied as I melted into Phil's settee.

"Okay, let me babble for a while. I'll keep an eye on the clock and tell you when you have to leave." I drifted into semi-unconsciousness and let his meanderings seep into me.

"Well, I suppose I could start with a few unwritten ball rules like:

1. Never jump out of the net and scream YES as it would freak everybody out.

2. Never swear at the ref because they will change balls immediately.

3. When put into the crowd, always bounce around happily because it is the fans that pay everyone's wage.

4. Try not to cause car accidents – so when bouncing down a road, always get on to the pavement as soon as possible.

"Not all balls like each other, you know. But just think of being stuck in a ball bag night after night with clever dick balls. Mind you, I have made some amazing friends, and lost a few. Did you know that 160 people get shot at football matches in Bolivia every year? In fact the British Consul in La Paz, which is the economic capital of Bolivia, got shot in the shoulder while sitting at his desk. Apparently some fan shot a gun in the air outside the British Embassy after a match and the bullet came down through the roof and embedded itself in this man's shoulder. But more importantly 300 balls get shot there – it's crazy. In fact a group of balls got together to form an action group but they all got put in positions where they got shot by a 'hit ball'. I think it was the Mafia from Santa Cruz that made the balls and because it is a small country, balls are money. On a lighter note one of the touch-line songs from there was the Bob Marley favourite, I SHOT THE REFEREE SO I COULD NOT TAKE THE PENALTY.

"Mind you they eat balls that win games in Papua New Guinea so as to take the spirit from the ball.

"We used to help each other in the locker rooms and had to educate young or new balls. I suppose it was a bit like your nurseries. I mean there was education. For example, one and one equals a draw – greater number wins on aggregate etc.

"There are nursery rhymes to get them into ball chants and at the same time teach morals and suchlike:
This little ball went to market
This little ball stayed at home
This little ball had a good game
And this little ball went bounce bounce bounce right out of the park.
OR
Little Miss Muffet sat on her tuffet
Bouncing her favourite ball
When down came three spiders that hung just beside her

And a neat back flick squashed them all.

"Are you still with me, Bren?"

"Yes." I was sniggering to myself. "I was just thinking about one and one equals a draw."

"Well, we could talk about the more serious aspects of balls, i.e. the universal concept of spheres."

"No, no!" I exclaimed. "But one thing that you have never talked about is other types of balls – you know, like do you ever watch television? Snooker for example?"

"Fuck off!" cried Granville. "Sorry for swearing but thinking of other balls in the same way as footballs makes you want to swear. Anyway snooker balls are so thick and dense, aren't they?"

"Well I suppose so – so what's your favourite television programme about balls apart from soccer?"

"Well, polo is too frightening – it reminds me of being in the middle of a motorway. Athletics have only got the shot put and they're more stupid than snooker balls. Cricket's good. It has pace, the angles and plenty of amazing possibilities. Tennis is crap and the balls definitely need a haircut to give the game pace. As for basketball, well those guys have just got too much bounce and they're just so full of it. All this 'Hey Granville man' and 'Just chill out and bounce' rubbish! I met a squash ball once but they just talk so fast – he just fizzed all over the place, totally hyperactive. That's what comes of smashing into walls all day."

"Yes, I'd rather be a football. However, we do have differences like yourselves; for example a country ball can get kicked out of its garden and go round the village for a few days and will always end up in its own garden. But a city ball that gets kicked out of its area will get mugged. City balls on average get stolen and sold at least five times in their lives."

I looked at the clock on the wall. It was time for me to go. I didn't know what to say. Granville started.

"Hey, Bren. Thanks for all the interaction. I know you have to go and we'll meet again. You'd best get off and rest your brain for a few days. C'mon, knickers and socks in the bag and out of that door!"

I did as I was told. I had twenty-five minutes to get the train. I wanted to stay – it really hurt.

Having packed, I walked to the door and turned and waved at Granville. I'm sure he was smiling. All I could say was, "Thanks – see you soon."

I locked up and ran down the stairs, out through the back garden to see the little face hanging on the fence.

"Have a good trip," this little squeaky voice said and I suddenly got an after-shock of incredible power and energy coming from the little brain. I darted down the street and caught Granville's last words of the day, "Don't go talking to strange balls!" then I was on my way home.

Chapter 6 – The Abduction

I arrived home very tired and mulled over what had happened in the last three days. I felt uncomfortable with my new skill acquisition and I had a lot to do, preparing for the next day, which was back to work. How can I prepare for work? Surely this new skill should be the talk of every radio and television show. I could be famous. I let this run past me for a while and then thought of all the people that are deemed crazy. I mean – if you talk to God, that's okay. But if you tell people that God is talking to you they call you mad, and will lock you up for a lot of years.

I performed as best as I could at work and seemed to go back to my old gentle self. I must admit that even if I was going crazy, I sure felt better.

Two weeks passed with me moving from my little house to work and back, with the occasional visit to a local fish and chip shop.

At the end of the fortnight I went in to work and asked for the two weeks holiday that was due to me. They owed me the time and allowed me to take the fortnight straight away.

I sat looking at the phone in my front room, part buried beneath a pile of sports books and magazines. Then I picked up the phone and rang Philip. As the phone was ringing I considered the reasons why Phil had not rung me; he thought I was cracking up, thought I was not his friend anymore or simply had not got time for me. This was a silly thought as he only rang me every blue moon!

He answered the phone like a long lost friend and gave me all the usual pleasantries. I detected something in his voice – he was avoiding something. I had to ask the question.

"Phil, is Granville okay?"

I got nothing but silence for what seemed like five minutes.

"Bren," he replied, "Granville isn't here anymore."

The words penetrated my gut instantly.

"What's happened?" I whispered.

"He's not here anymore. I went out to the garden the day after you left, and had left him under the tree as normal. At tea time when I returned, he was gone."

I didn't know what to say. I felt upset and uncomfortable. I questioned him a little more and could get nothing out of him other than he was glad I rang because he hadn't the heart to ring me and tell me.

"Look, Phil. Can I come down for a day or two, just to clear the air and gather myself?" I asked.

"Sure, that's what friends are for. Come anytime you like."

"I'll be on the train tomorrow. I'll be there by midday. Okay?"

Phil agreed to leave the key in the normal place and not forget this time. He was great. He said he would get some food in and a nice bottle of brandy and told me to occupy myself with writing.

I seemed to wait forever for the time to come round when I was turning into the street of Phil's flat. I found the key, walked in and found a lovely note from Phil. It read;

Bren my dear friend – I hope you had a good journey and have arrived safely. Do not worry yourself about Granville and the events that happened last time you were here. It's OUR problem because I am your friend and will always be, so chin up and just mellow out and let me take as much of the burden as you want.

See you later. By the way, help yourself – mi casa su casa.

A big hug
Phil

I started to feel better. I don't normally drink during the day except if there is a match on, but I poured a healthy brandy and went for a slow mooch round the garden. I stared at the tree for a while.

The little head pulled itself up over the fence, and the little squeaky voice said, "I've been waiting for you! Get your arse round here."

I had that surge of being around a great power again. It didn't take me long to climb over the fence to find myself in an ordinary street, well, cul-de-sac really. They looked like council houses, all fronted with reasonable sized gardens and low walls at the front. My little head was sitting on the wall on the left-hand side with the body of an adult, but about three feet shorter than normal. His little legs were crossed and he was in the process of rolling a cigarette. He looked upset, yet seemingly in incredible control of everything in his immediate space.

I wandered across with my brandy, sat next to him and waited for him to speak. He put out his little hand to mine.

"Josh McGuinness at your service," he said. "So you've come for Granville have you, Bren?"

"Yes, and how do you know my name?"

"Granville told me, and he has been abducted."

"Abducted! What do you mean?"

"Very simple, my friend," he squeaked. "You see the house across the road with all the cars in the drive?"

"Yes."

"Well the day after you left, that family had visitors from London. Their visitors had a young boy about ten years old and he was playing cricket with the people's kids who live here and their cricket ball went over into Phil's garden. The Londoner jumped over and came back with Granville as well. I live in the house next door and heard Granville talking to himself about possibilities in London and thought that was strange. So I came out to find him being put in the back of the car. He was practising cockney accents. When everyone from that house had gone in for tea, I wandered along and sat on their wall and reminded Granville of how little time left he had on this earth."

"What!" I winced. "What exactly do you mean about little time left?" My heart started pounding.

He grabbed my wrist with one hand and started to tap my other wrist with his other hand.

"Don't speak," he said gently. "Just squeeze my wrist, the one that is not tapping. Squeeze it to the beat of my taps."

I followed his instruction and after thirty seconds felt my heart slowing down. I felt calm. In fact the last time I was so calm was when I cooked half an ounce of cannabis into a curry by mistake.

"Listen carefully. I know you are a ball psychic. I know you are one of Granville's students. Granville has a remarkable personality and great patience and sensitivity towards others. He's helped me in too many ways to go into, but as well as being ball psychic, I am also a true dreamer."

"A what?"

"A true dreamer. This means that every now and then I have dreams that come true. I can sometimes control it; what I mean is I can think of a person and will myself to dream about them and I will. Well, not long after I met Granville I had a dream about his death within the next few weeks. It would be in somewhere strange to me. A place with what looked like aboriginal designs on the ground. The problem I have is that Granville is shouting for you at the top of his voice. I have never heard him shout like that. It frightened me. So, there you have it – you have to be there when he goes!"

I still felt calm but sad.

"What do I do?"

"His last message to me, before he was taken in the car with the visitors to the train station, was to tell you to follow his trail and use the ball network."

"Where has he gone, and how do I do it?"

"Well he was taken to London Euston – that's all I know. As for the networking bit, you have to do what I do, just keep moving around until you make contact with a ball psychic or a ball. They all have brilliant memories and notice everything that is going on. Follow the yellow ball road." He sang at the end and his voice changed into the smoothest alto range you had ever heard.

"No!" he corrected himself, this time not singing. "Follow the blue ball road – think blue if you want to make psychic connections. Yellow is for the nervous system and calming states."

I felt as though the whole world was opening and becoming bigger and more complicated. I thanked him.

"Cheers, Josh, and go to your careers officer about music college. You will be brilliant as a singer."

"Yes, thanks to you I already have and my name is really Marion Longbottom. Josh is my front to make me look taller."

I laughed. "Well I think Josh McGuinness will be a brilliant stage name. Hang on. How did you know I was going to say this?"

"I dreamed it – dreamed this meeting we are having now. Look, Bren, you've got to go and get on the next train to London."

"Yes, I suppose I have," I replied.

I left him sitting on his low wall with his legs swinging, singing to himself.

I went back to Phil's flat at a steady pace. I knew I was going to London. I had the holiday money and credit cards, yet I didn't seem to rush. I was purposeful in everything I did to get to London except the note for Phil, which read.

Phil – I know where Granville is!
I've gone to London. Don't know how long it will take me. It's all been dreamt before you know!! Amazing.
I think Granville's dying. I'll keep in touch. Thanks for your support I knew you would understand.
Ps. I have given your bottle of brandy to the little head to help with loosening his vocal chords in readiness for fame.
Think of the possibilities – anything could happen!
Bren

I did get the next train to London. What will happen? No accommodation, I didn't know where I was going.

I sat on the train and thought of Granville, then thought of all the strange balls I might meet. The anorak in me started coming out as I mused about London teams and the grounds I'd visited there. Highbury, White Hart Lane, the old Plough Lane when Wimbledon were still there, even Barnet's decrepit Underhill. I wondered what names London balls might have when I encountered them. Peter Osgood? George Graham? Terry Venables possibly? Or what about Bertie Mee? A grin spread across my face thinking about the way Arsenal's double-winning manager had been immortalised in a rude piece of Cockney rhyming slang. I wouldn't be able to keep a straight face if I came across a ball named after Bertie.

London clubs weren't my favourite teams generally, though like a lot of supporters I had a quiet regard for West Ham. Lots of fans used to feel like that about them because they had the wit to play cultured football and the good grace to lose most of their away games. Mind you, that was a Sixties and Seventies thing really. Makes you feel a bit old.

I've got a clear memory of a League Cup semi in 1972 and West Ham playing Stoke City. A muddy pitch glistening in the floodlights and Stoke awarded a vital penalty. The keeper must have been injured (never sent off in those days before the flurry of red cards) because the late, great Bobby Moore had to go in goal for it. And he saved it! But the ball came back to the Stoke player and he booted it in. Typical West Ham – style in defeat, losing to a team that had never appeared at Wembley before or since.

Next up was a cup-tie in 1976 between Chelsea – (always a glamour club) – and lowly Orient. The minnows won it with a glorious shot from outside the area by a hitherto unknown full-back called Bill Roffey. I might have forgotten many more gifted players but not Bill because for years afterwards at our school any pile-driver strike was always given the epithet a 'Bill Roff'.

Thinking of Chelsea got me thinking about their name.

When they were founded they could have been called 'Kensington' or even 'London FC'. Bet Ken Bates wished they had plumped for that option. I was pulled out of this reverie because the train was slowing and people were stirring; also a young girl was staring at me because I'd had my eyes closed and a grin on my face.

The first station we pulled into was Coventry; as we pulled in slowly I heard a strange conversation going on in my head. It was two local balls having a debate about Coventry City's recent home defeat by Southampton. The Sky Blues were already looking at yet another relegation battle and losing to the Saints – potential fellow strugglers – was a major blow.

I interrupted them and said, "Allow me to introduce myself. I'm Bren, a friend of the ball Granville Tingate. Sorry to interrupt, but have you heard of him and has he passed this way?"

"Where are you? Oh my name is Jimmy Hill and my ball friend is Keith Houchen."

"I'm on the train. Where are you?"

"We're above your head, stuck in the roof rafters of the station. We've been here two and a half years. Yes, Granville passed through a few days ago. He seemed a thoroughly decent sort of ball. He did, however, say that he was going to have a rough ride, because he had just been abducted by a family of London gangsters and didn't expect much time left as they tend to abuse balls."

"Is that all he said?"

"Yes, sorry."

The train started to pull out. I thanked them both briefly and asked, if I should be back in the area, would they like to be set free from the rafters. They thanked me but declined the offer as they thought their lifestyle was exciting –

getting all the conversations from all the different travellers. I could see their point; after all everyone says that train stations are interesting places.

I started to feel uncomfortable again and tried to narrow down all the London clubs that have connections with gangsters. It seemed a useless task though because how can you get a club to admit it's got gangsters among the fans? I mean, you get the odd whisper now and then but nothing really concrete; probably you'd know more if you lived in the capital. Crooks are just like everyone else when it comes to sport. Some of them are only attracted to winners and hang about the glam clubs while others stick to a local side they were brought up with through thick and thin. Generally, they don't see much benefit in getting involved financially, too much scrutiny. That's in this country, but in South America it can be different. Colombian soccer is dominated by drug barons who looked on clubs as a useful way of laundering dirty money. And Maradona got very close to the Camorra in Naples when he played there, so they say.

The nearest I could think of in Britain was Stan Flashman at Barnet but he wasn't a gangster, just a sort of super tout. There didn't seem a way to take things further without getting some more information from a ball in the know.

The train pushed on a bit further and I took a walk for a sandwich and can of beer. On the way back, right at the beginning of coach D, a voice said, "Where ye gangin', like?"

Straight away I knew it was a ball from the Newcastle area. I scanned the seats and saw him amongst a crowd of what can only be described as brick shithouses with jeans and tee shirts on. I leant against the doorway and told him of my problems. He kept acknowledging my story with "Aye, canny" or "There's away". I knew I had time to spare so asked him what was new at Newcastle. He told me his name was George Robledo. I had to have a bit of a think about that one and he told me that this was one of a pair of brothers with Chilean passports who played for Newcastle in the Fifties.

"He's building a grand team ya knaw," said George, praising Keegan. "We'll soon be kicking the Mancs oot o' top spot."

"I know. I saw them at Villa a couple of weeks back and they looked very solid."

"Aye, that was a canny win. There was bit ale supped after that one I can tell yer."

The conversation came to an abrupt end. I had not realised it but as I was talking to George I had started leaning towards him, cocking my head, nodding and smiling. The ball was in the lap of one of the brick shithouses and he had noticed what I was looking at and got the wrong end of the stick.

I moved from coach D to coach M faster than the train was going.

The train pulled into Euston after a twenty-minute wait in a tunnel. I had visions of being raped and pillaged by the shithouses whilst we were waiting. Where had all that fire and energy gone from when I was with Granville? I started to think about the brain and how it worked. Where was my mad monkey when I needed it?

We eventually pulled in and I had already decided to go to a coffee bar on the station and take stock of the situation. I sat down on one of those high stools. I had a good view of all the station and the platforms. I could hear two voices outside of all the rabble and faintly caught a conversation. Who was it? It wasn't Granville, that's for sure. It was a very strange conversation, almost like an interrogation. I cast my eyes round and pin-pointed it to two people sitting on a bench. An old lady, the typical stereotype grandma with brown overcoat and little round hat, sitting next to a young boy of about twelve dressed in school uniform with his hands wrapped tightly round a ball.

I moved across the station with my coffee and the words grew stronger.

"If you do not tell me what will happen with Millwall and Brentford on Saturday I will pour petrol over you tonight and that will be you gone. I only earned ten quid last week through my bets and you said you would help me, so no more fifty-fifty chances. I want some winners and I want them now!" said the small boy.

The ball stuttered a reply. Then the strangest thing happened. I stood frozen to the spot and was forced to turn slowly by an unseen force. My eyes nearly jumped out of their sockets. IT WAS CATTY!

She stood there, a few feet in front of me with a smile as wide as the Amazon. My body went into wobbly jelly mode, and all I could do was smile back. She walked towards me through the noise and smells – she simply seemed to cut through it all as though she was a walking dream. Then reality hit.

"C'mon Bren, we've no time to lose!" She grabbed my jacket collar and turned me to face a train on platform six. "We have to get that train and it's ready to go. C'mon!"

"Why?" I coughed and spluttered as I was marched across the end of the platforms.

"Because I know where Granville has gone, and we have to move quickly – he's not in London!"

I realised what was happening and as we passed the grandma and her grandson I suddenly pulled Catrina to one side. "How long have we got?"

"Two minutes."

"Right, I am going to cause a distraction. You see that ball in the young lad's lap?"

"Yes."

"I want that ball on the train with us .You grab it and I'll see you on the train."

With that I walked towards the young boy, pretended to trip and threw my now cold coffee over him and the grandma. I started apologising and Catty sneaked in and grabbed the ball. The lad was quick to give chase to Catty so she ran round the platform ends and shot down number three. I ran towards the train on six. Catty had done a U-turn and was running down three parallel to me.

"Bren!" she screamed then took a perfect goalie four step run up and sliced the ball, sending it over three sets of lines, curving round to land in my arms. She jumped onto the empty tracks and hopped her way across. This was too scary for the boy and we jumped on to the train. We entered the coach to a mixture of applause with "Nice kick" and "You've broke that boy's heart."

"Thank you," said Catrina to the smiling ones.

"Fuck off!" said I to the miserable ones.

We moved down the coaches, sat down, and spent the next couple of minutes in silence catching our breath.

I thought, 'where are we going? Is this the same Catrina as the last one I met? Who the hell is sitting in my lap?'

The first reply was from the ball. He said, "Th-Thank you for getting me away from that child. I-I'm Ossie Ardiles."

He had quite a faint voice but we both heard him. I was

about to ask about his name when he interrupted.

"I'm called Ossie Ardiles because the other balls reckon my English is about as good as his was when he first came to the UK. On acc-account of my stutter you s-see. Also I come from North London near the Tot-Tot-Tot Spurs ground. I don't mind though because I like having the name of such a famous p-p-p-player."

"Granville mentioned you once. He'd never met you but he's heard about a ball that was renowned for predicting the results of matches before they even started. That was you wasn't it?"

"I've got some talent for that, but I'm not the only one," he replied modestly.

The second answer was "Edinburgh," as confirmed by the customer announcement.

The third was, "Yes it is me, Catrina, and I have changed, and I am still changing I think?"

"Well, what's happened?" I couldn't wait for her to fill me in.

"Okay. That phone conversation we had when I was dumped by Phil? I realised something was different in the conversation. I couldn't put my finger on it until a ball from my local team that I support spoke to me. It really scared me at first."

"Your local team? Who, why?"

"My team's Charlton. I haven't lived near the ground for years but my granddad was a big fan – he used to go in the days when you could get 70,000 into the Valley. He was even there for the famous game when they lost 6-5 after being 5-1 up with 20 minutes left. When I came along he used to take me, especially as I haven't got any brothers. I didn't go so much when I was older; but then we had all this trouble about losing the Valley and the club folding, and like a lot of others I rallied round when they were threatened and I've been back into it ever since. I even stood for the election on the supporters' ticket when we took on the local council to let us back into the Valley.

"I never really mentioned it to Phil because at heart he doesn't really fancy the idea of a woman who knows as much about football as he does. Thinks he likes the idea but when it comes down to it if you show some awareness he feels threatened by it. And anyway, he's a glory hunter; latched on to Liverpool when he doesn't even come from there. I get sick of hearing him bang on about Dalglish and 'knocking it' and the Inter Milan back four – he's a soccer snob.

"But let me tell you about Granville. I was at last Saturday's match at the Valley and really enjoying it when Granville spoke to me from one of the private boxes. He told me about the abduction and said you would be looking for him, and that it had all been dreamed before. I didn't understand it all at first and still don't now. Anyway Granville was swapped with friends of the gangsters to another gangster crowd from Edinburgh, and left for Scotland last Tuesday. I'll tell you, Bren, I don't know what's happening but this is the most exciting thing that has happened to me!"

"Well I've got a couple of weeks off so I have the time to search. What about you?"

"Oh I don't really work. I do a bit for my father because he's chief editor of the Evening Standard. Anyway, I don't really need to work. I'll just give daddy a ring and tell him I will be seeing friends in Edinburgh. I do have some friends there where we can stay. They're really nice people. Gemma who's a top management consultant and her boyfriend is Alex who's a session musician, trumpeter."

"Very nice," I said with a cynical edge.

" Oh, you will like Alex. He collects single malt whisky and drinks a lot of it too."

"Okay so I go with Alex to get drunk and you go with Gemma to talk big money and business."

"No, not now. I've changed. We'll drink the malt and you can join us. Gemma won't take any arm bending."

At that moment she curled her arm under mine and squeezed it gently. I suddenly felt like I was a child and got my first date. My mind started making assumptions about her move.

"Does this mean we are 'together'?" I asked.

"Depends on what you mean by together?" she replied and laughed.

"I mean, can we work as a team to find Granville – you know share everything and one hundred percent commitment?"

"You start the commitment and I'll join in," she replied with a powerful confidence.

"Let's talk about the match with you and Granville. What happened and were there many ball conversations?"

"Yes, it was a real revelation. The match was a pretty good one as well because Derby look like a good bet for promotion this year. It finished 2-2 and there was plenty of incident, but the best bit came when Granville struck up a conversation with one of the balls from Derby. Can you guess his name?"

I frowned a bit and she decided to help me out.

"The most famous person connected with Derby County?"

"Brian Clough?"

"Spot on. And he behaved like him as well! When some of the other balls were blurting out a few risqué chants he was straight in with, 'Gentlemen let's keep the swearing down please'. And he'd got strong ideas on how the game should be played; spent a lot of time berating the Derby forwards as a bunch of jessies and asking the winger if he understood what his job was – not that the winger could hear him of course. Some of the other balls call him 'Big Mouth' but that doesn't seem to bother him much and we got on quite well once he stopped calling me 'young lady'. Apparently, because of the famous name there's another ball who likes to be called Brian Clough as well and as you can imagine they don't exactly hit it off, but 'Brian 2' wasn't at the game because his owner left him in a garage in Belper."

"Sounds like this Cloughie was quite a character."

"Oh he certainly was. He and Granville engaged in some really deep conversation about the effects of changes to the offside law and the back pass rule on the modern game. Cloughie compared it to the 1920s when they took away the requirement to have three players between the attacker and goal and so full backs couldn't play offside so readily. Granville seemed to agree with him but most of it went over my head."

"And the ball chants?" I asked.

"Well there was, 'Ramming along at the baseball honey' (to the tune of Mungo Jerry), 'One goal for haddocks, It's just one goal for haddocks' (to the tune of Guantalamera), and for when they lost, 'I haddock a dream' (ABBA).

"Also, it is well known that about 160 lorry drivers use Jim Smith's nickname as a CB handle. All over Derbyshire you can tune in to 'Bald Eagles'!"

It was early evening when we passed through Newcastle. We both scanned the station for balls. Catrina caught one and said hello and that I had met George Robledo and had nearly got myself into trouble with the shithouses. The ball, who called himself Rob Lee, said that he knew of them and that they were real hardcore Toon Army; the type of guys who go to matches in just the strip whatever the weather. In his opinion the North-East contained the maddest fans in the country, both Newcastle and Sunderland. He had this theory that really they were more like Scots than the rest of England and he went into a long explanation about Scots invasions of England to back it up. In his view only the Scots could top the North-East for fanaticism. It wasn't a comforting thought given where we were heading.

Chapter 7 – Across The Border

We entered Berwickshire and I commented on Berwick upon Tweed.

"Berwick was part of Scotland for a long time and it only came back after a punitive expedition by the Duke of Gloucester in around 1480-odd. He went on to be Richard III of ill-repute," I added.

Catty suppressed a yawn and I decided I'd better change tack.

"Ironic because they're the only English side playing in the Scottish League."

"Like Gretna playing in the English pyramid," she shot back.

"Now that's impressive," I said with admiration.

"B-Brilliant," agreed Ossie.

She smiled and said we were a right pair of anoraks but I could see she was pleased. Her body moved a bit closer to prove it.

We sped through towards Edinburgh, past the links and cliffs, and we had a good conversation with our new-found friend laying in my lap.

We arrived at Waverley station. I had never been before, so left it up to Catrina to be the guide. We jumped off the train and I started walking towards the taxi rank.

"No," said Catty, "we walk up the rise and get one off the streets, it's faster. We'll get a taxi to Gemma's because it's getting late and we can start afresh in the morning."

It worked a treat. We jumped into a cab.

"Will they mind us just rolling up?"

"No. I rang on my mobile when you went to the toilet earlier. I caught Gemma on her second gin and tonic, so she was really receptive. We'll no doubt go to their local for a night cap drink."

"Where's the local?"

"Well it's round the back of the castle sort of. Tollcrossish. Gilmore Place to be exact and there's the castle."

"Wow!" I said, but couldn't help let the football get the better of me. I asked the taxi driver, "Who do you support?"

"A wife and three kids. How about you?"

"No. I mean football."

"Are you a Jambo?"

Catrina jumped in. "Yes we are, what happened last week?" (Jambos are Hearts supporters – jamb tarts!)

"You might ask," spat the driver. "Beat 2-1 at the Bairns." He shook his head.

I shot Catty a quizzical look but she was floundering too.

"F-Falkirk," interjected Ossie

"That's no' the sort of game we should be losing if we're going to challenge for Europe. Robertson scored but the others, well…"

He took one hand off the wheel to make a Roman Emperor thumbs-down motion.

As we got out and paid the fare, he concluded with, "Well, hen, we'll see you at Tynecastle next week?"

"Yes maybe," Catrina replied and said goodbye.

"Maybe it's me, Catty, but he hardly acknowledged me at all. Does he fancy you?"

"No. But what you have to understand about the Scots is that I made the play about Hearts, not you. So he talks to the one who knows. There's no gender issues in Scottish football – just a recognition of a fan, whatever they are."

"Tell me more about Scottish football."

"Later," she replied and held my hand while ringing the doorbell. I felt as though I was young again and being taken to the zoo.

We were taken in to a typical greystone Edinburgh building but the art inside was like a gallery. Gemma and Alex showed incredible courtesy and broke down all formalities with two swift gin and tonics and a dram of Talisker single malt. A quick wash and we were out. Down the road into Bennet's. What a pub! Alex introduced me to a couple of pints of 80 shillings and Gemma introduced me to some local characters.

Gemma was not at all like I expected. She was funny, stimulating and had eyes that lit up like candles. Alex was a shock. I expected a musician who would talk nothing but music. I don't think he ever mentioned music once. Yet he had a story for every twist and turn of our conversation. Towards the end of the night both Gemma and Alex couldn't resist asking why we had come without any change of clothes, and pointed out they had plenty and we could stay as long as we liked. Catty and I looked each other and nodded.

We told them everything in a fast babble that lasted five minutes.

Gemma's response was that she could get us in to most places in Edinburgh if it would help. After saying that she wanted the conversation to return to normal. I don't think she was convinced.

Alex's response was amazing. He said he'd heard of these balls and people, and told us of unusual things that had happened to his friends. He then talked about the great silkie and the term shape-shifter took on a new meaning.

Granville was to all intents and purposes an inanimate object. Had the Scots been doing this for years with mother earth? Alex went all broody and Gemma was a little disturbed.

"C'mon Alex," Gemma said. "You know what happened last time. You went out one day and lost two and a half weeks of your life with the Stone of Destiny! And you still will not tell me what happened."

Alex smiled, leant over and asked, "Is this a mission?"

"Yes," I replied.

"Then I'll help. I'm in between contracts and have a few days free."

We moved round the corner to Burlington Berties, a pub just opposite the stage door to the King's Theatre. Here we made some more friends and had some more drinks.

We ended the evening by Alex telling us exactly when to cross the road without getting run over. I didn't realise Edinburgh was such a lively place.

I don't know how it happened but Catty and I ended up in the same bed and we both must have fallen fast asleep. The next morning I woke up with my nose gently resting on Cattys' nose. I savoured the moment and then Alex crashed through into the bedroom demanding that we get up if we were to start the mission.

We borrowed what bits of clothing we could and fell downstairs, to meet Alex fighting with a frying pan and Gemma making seemingly world-shattering important calls. We fed and washed up.

"Right," said Alex, "we have people to talk to! C'mon Bren."

With that, we went off at a brisk walk towards the centre and veered right behind the castle. Alex mumbled all the way about where these people would be and what the reception would be like. We eventually arrived at a tenement block and Alex rang the flat bell.

"It's Alex – is that David Bowie?"

I heard a rumble of vocal chords that I couldn't make out and the door lock opened. We walked through the hall past any array of multicoloured umbrellas, all with their bases stuck into huge plant pots.

"Is he really David Bowie?" I asked.

"No, they've all have taken famous names in this tenement. It's quite well known around here that it is full of people who are like shadows in the night." At that moment someone passed as we were walking upstairs.

"Morning John." Alex nodded. And the man returned the greeting.

"John who?" I asked.

"John Lee Hooker, of course."

I laughed, as the man that had just passed had bright red hair, a black heavy metal tee shirt and a brilliant green tartan kilt.

We arrived at David Bowie's door and knocked. This wiry person stuck his head out sheepishly and recognised Alex. He then nodded to Alex while his eyes were fixed on me.

"This is Bren, he's a big man from down south."

The door opened and we walked into the English Royal Mint – there were hundreds of five, ten and twenty-pound notes littered around the room. My mouth opened wide; Alex caught sight of me and laughed, then spoke in what I later found out to be a Morningside accent.

"You will notice that he only copies English pound notes."

David grunted, "Well it disnae fucking matter cos oors

isnae legal tender oanywaye."

We sat down and had a cup of green tea. David and Alex obviously had news to catch up on, then he started questioning David.

"I wonder if you can help – I want know where there is the most saturation of footballs in the city, and also of any connections with gangsters?"

I thought this was a strange way of questioning, because David had not been told of anything. I soon learned that in Scotland any question is taken seriously and that you don't ask why but simply do the best to answer it. I thought this must be the reason why there have been so many inventors to come out of this country. I was starting to think like Granville again.

"And can these balls be geographically linked to Waverley station?" I chipped in.

"Brilliant question!" David said as he picked his teeth with the end of a knife. "I would say Gorgie or Roseburn Road area because they all leave them in the fucking yards and greens they never garden – so lots must get lost in the jungles. Some of the big finance companies support the Jambos and where there is big money there are gangsters. The trick is how to link to Waverley station."

'Brilliant', I thought, this was like what Granville told me. What did he call it – nomological deduction? It's like if you want to find the best dentist in a new town you simply visit all the receptions and see which one has the most worn-out carpet. 'This guy is good', I thought.

Alex remained quiet and gave David thinking time. I was impressed with how the Scots never interrupt. Mind you, Catrina has Scottish blood and she constantly interrupted me on the train yesterday.

David spoke. "Bus routes!" he exclaimed, "because you

often see Hearts supporters carrying balls on buses going back and forward from the city and Waverley is at the end of Princes Street – how about that for this time in the morning?"

"That's nae bad," said Alex whilst slightly bowing his head. "Shall we follow this idea, Bren?"

"Yes," I replied, not knowing the areas they were talking about. Alex then had a quick conversation with David about who they knew of in Hearts supporters.

We left and took a brisk walk, or should I say a brisk climb. This city is all hills. We arrived at Waverley station.

"Well it's up to you now," Alex said and started talking to nearly everyone in the city. I remembered Gemma telling me the night before that she hates walking with Alex as he never gets more than ten steps without talking to someone he knows. Her trick apparently was to keep on walking; he would stop and have a brief conversation, then see Gemma disappearing round a corner, running to catch her up – a bit like a dog and its owner.

I mooched round the platforms and opened up my mind.

It was on platform nineteen that I got contact. A ball was muttering to itself in a mid-Yorkshire accent.

"Ayup!" I said.

"Ayup there!" the ball replied. The ball was actually in Princess Street Gardens but had been wedged next to the railway fencing. After a brief conversation he informed me that he was originally from York and had been brought on a day out. He desperately wanted to get back to York.

"Look, have your ever heard of Granville Tingate?"

"Fuck off, everyone's heard of the Yorkshire ball of the stars!"

"Recently?"

"Yes, last week, I think – we only had a few seconds and

you know how long the introductions can take."

"Well, what did he say?"

"He said he had been abducted and first went to London and now was heading for Gorgie Road."

"Brilliant!"

"Hey, could you do me a favour? There's a York train due on this platform in a couple of minutes. Could you throw me on and ask someone to kick me out at York station?"

"Yeah, sure."

I looked for Alex and saw him talking to a young couple at the end of the platform. I ran to him and explained that we had a small mission. I told him I was going to run out of the station, into Princess Street Gardens and throw him a football; he had to wait at the other end of the platform. His orders were to jump on to the train, give it to someone going past York and ask them to throw it out at York.

I ran round, got hold of the ball and cracked it with the side of my foot to send it over the lines and along platform nineteen towards Alex. The train arrived within seconds and I saw Alex jump on and move along the coaches. He made contact with a businessman in a suit. The man nodded and put the ball under his briefcase. Then the train rolled off. I shouted bye to the ball and suddenly thought, "What's your name?"

"Joe Pepper," he called, "what's yours?"

I told him and then he was out of range.

I strolled through the station feeling very smug. I met and explained to Alex what happened. He looked impressed but baffled.

I said "C'mon, I'll get you a coffee and if there is a ball around I'll do something to give you proof. Anyway, how did you convince the businessman?"

"Simple. He is a banker from Perth. I just asked him if he was a true Scot and told him it was a mission to do with the Stone of Destiny – he would have hand-delivered it if you had wanted."

"What's with this Stone of Destiny?"

"It's supposed to be in Westminster Abbey, where it was put after Edward 1 stole it away. The real one is hidden in Scotland where it has always been, but most Scots don't know where and are trying to get Edward's thieved one back!"

We went and sat down in an open area of the station and had coffee. The station was 'hoachin' with furriners!' according to Alex which meant full of tourists. I asked him to visually scan for a ball. There were two different parties with balls. Alex laughed and said he knew the couple with the young lad about twenty yards to our left. I told him I would try and link up.

"Hello there, having a nice day?" I focused hard on the ball sat on the lap of the father.

"You must be jokin'. We're away t' Spain for two weeks but this daft bastard podgered his wife's sister last week to try to get him to take her on holiday as well. And, he knows she'll tell his wife when we get back because he couldn't afford it."

I passed a few pleasantries and asked him who he supported. Hibs was the answer and apparently this is going to be a cracking season for the Easter Road boys. One of the best since World War Two, so the ball said, as long as Darren Jackson stayed fit. He asked me, did I know that Hibs were the first British side to play in the European Cup but then Hibs supporters tend to say that to everyone. I've met Hibees fans before. Nonetheless, the ball seemed surprised that a sassenach would know it.

I finished with, "Where do you live, what are your names?"

I shut off and relayed to Alex.

"He's called James McDuff, and she is called Mary; the ball's called Alex Cropley. They live at what sounded like Bruntsfield Links? And there will be a riot when they get back off holiday because James podgered his wife's sister in the Meadows last week."

Alex burst out laughing then suddenly swung round to me and said, "That's fucking amazing – fucking amazing!"

"What's podgering?" I asked.

"When do you get sex education classes in England?"

The penny dropped and I felt out of touch.

"Hey, let's go and visit my bank manager," exclaimed Alex.

"I need him to have a ball," I replied.

"That's true, they don't have balls do they?"

We jollied around for a few minutes then decided to take a bus and continue the search.

I don't know where we went, but we ended up a couple of streets from an incredibly large stadium. We hopped off.

"Is that the Hearts ground?" I asked.

Alex gave me a look of disgust and said, "I'll forgive you this once – that's the Holy Ground."

"What?"

"It's Murrayfield! Tynecastle is a little further up – let's go into this pub."

We went into the Roseburn.

Alex ordered and I paid – that was the deal. He would take me everywhere if I paid, because technically he was out of work. Or at least that's how he figured it; musicians are skint and out of work when they are not playing.

We had a couple of pints for lunch and Alex did the

main talking. Nothing much was gained. We decided to walk around the streets whilst I looked into gardens, down alleys, into back yards, or greens as they're called.

We seemed to move away from Tynecastle and get nearer to Murrayfield, then it all happened at once. About twenty incredibly hard Scottish voices talking so broad that I couldn't understand filled my head. They weren't talking about football! They were talking about rugby!

I said to Alex, "I think I've just made contact with all the rugby balls inside Murrayfield!"

Alex looked at me and the blood drained from his face. "What are they saying?"

"That Scotland can win the Five Nations next season, but if they don't, it's important to beat the English as they haven't won since that Grand Slam decider in 1990. They're betting each other about the outcome of the 1995 World Cup and most of them are arguing for either New Zealand or Australia.

I asked to speak to one ball, and asked for its name.

"Gavin Hastings," came the reply. What a full-back that man is! The ball was suitably impressed that I admired Big Gav.

"Look, I know it may be an awkward question but have you heard of a football called Granville Tingate?"

"Hang on, I'll ask around." I heard what was like a herd of buffalos talking, then the amazing reply came.

"He's at the Tynecastle ground and when you see him tell him to keep the noise down."

"Brilliant, I'll have a walk over."

"Hang on – I've just been told they're away training, including the balls. I think there is a midweek match tonight."

"Well, many thanks – anything I can do for you?"

"Yeah, find out what's going on in the English camp and fax it through to the real Gavin Hastings. Don't worry he's ball psychic. Me and him are a well known pair. He used to kick the ball high and I would put a certain type of spin on as I reached maximum height and this would create an ice layer. Only Gavin could catch me because other players would just drop me – there is a saying that at Murrayfield he would kick the ball so high that it would come down with snow on it. Don't believe it, it's fantasy. The reality is ice layers form a working partnership. Yes, we have barged through many a hotel door without opening it in the olden days…"

I laughed, and thought, this world is getting bigger and stranger by the minute. Alex couldn't resist chipping in to say hello to the balls. They heard him and surprised him by saying they had heard of his trumpeting and would ensure that he played at a celebratory party. Alex was impressed and asked if you get paid from balls.

We made our exit. Alex asked me about the gangster connection and I couldn't give him an answer. I said it was typical of these balls with big personalities. You just were constantly amazed at what they got up to.

Alex suggested we head back home and work out a plan for abducting Granville from Tynecastle.

On the way back I asked Alex if tickets were easy to get and should we get them now. Alex said that Gemma had contacts and we should make her work on the mission too.

Upon arriving home we found Gemma and Catrina sitting in the back garden sipping white wine. I blurted out our findings while Alex made sandwiches. Gemma and Catty just smiled in a very unsurprised way.

"Well thanks for that information, Bren, but we already knew and have made arrangements for the match tonight."

"Have you got tickets?" I begged.

Gemma looked at Catty and gave her a nod of approval to allow her to speak.

"Better than that, we will be in a private box."

"How did you do that?"

Gemma sat and gloated like the Queen of Sheba while Catty explained.

"Well, we started by sitting and thinking of what we knew. Edinburgh, gangsters, etc. We worked out that there are no real gangsters as such in this city, but it is the city of finance, and financiers talk like gangsters with take-over bids and taking out the opposition. The best connection we could come up with was Tynecastle who are sponsored by bankers and finance groups. So Gemma made a few calls and the results were startling. It is confidential but there are going to be some take-over bids with Scotland finance and banking taking over English finance and banking. It's all hush hush at the moment. Hence the London connection. So, Gemma found out that there is a contingent from the Tynecastle fans that are renowned for their predictions of games – a select few and most people that know of them think it is the whisky. So Gemma's contact has a private box at Tynecastle and we'll get some answers there!"

They both sat looking very smug and had a sip of wine. Alex caught the end of the conversation and said, "But do you know we know where Granville is? And did you know that James McDuff podgered his wife's sister last week?"

Catty was shocked and Gemma was disgusted at James McDuff.

We sat around in the garden for a couple of hours planning the abduction. I said to Catty that all these important and famous people were coming into my life. She agreed and confided to me that she was famous at one time in Edinburgh.

"What for?" I asked.

"I'm the one who fell off the balcony at the Fleetwood Mac concert when I was a student at the university here."

I noticed her hair was longer than when I originally met here and commented on how nice it looked.

The plan was to get in the private box. I was to make contact with Granville and at half-time go and join the spectators in the stand. Our contact would be talked into introducing the remainder to the team after the match (Catty would use her power to find a blackmailing edge) and Alex would grab Granville and kick him to me in the stands. I would leg it out and meet them later. Gemma would apologise for my behaviour and tell him that I was a grounds collector freak.

Simple.

Chapter 8 – The Second Abduction

Off we went to Tynecastle by taxi. It was horrific. The driver had his own personal mobile and started to have an argument with his wife, increasing his speed all the time. I could see that a few hundred yards in front someone was overtaking the other way and he was not going to slow down. I braced myself and within ten yards our driver pulled onto the pavement and started really laying into his wife about bank accounts and how much they did not have. The other driver stopped and came across to have a fight. Our driver carried on whilst opening the window to see what this guy wanted, oblivious to what was going on. The other driver listened for a second or two and thought he had better retire gracefully.

We carried on and Alex pointed out that it was so funny in taxis that everyone leans forward to talk to the driver, yet the microphone is just behind the back door so the driver always has to say speak up. I thought of this and, in the light of what had just happened, thought we had better keep quiet.

I was so thrilled at the thought of speaking to Granville. I wondered what he would say? It was at that point that I noticed Catty had a large plastic bag with her. I thought, sandwiches maybe as we had not had a proper meal for twenty-four hours.

"Sandwiches?" I asked.

"No, it's our little friend who we rescued from London."

"Bloody hell, I'd forgotten about him." I tried to connect

to Ossie and apologise but he had switched off and would not entertain me.

We went for a pre-match pint at the McLeod Street pub and then went into the stadium. I was impressed. It had a sort of compressed feeling to it. Great vision. I was introduced to a scotch pie and liked it. So I went back and had another. Unlike the one at Villa Park, I could tell what was in it and it didn't collapse.

I found out that there is a saying at Tynecastle – they have never lost a mid-week match if it's blowing a gale and throwing it down. I must admit lots of Jambos were looking up to the sky, seemingly praying for rain and wind.

We were introduced to Chris and his private box. He was really funny and regaled us with stories of the Jambos.

The match started. In all the excitement I realised that I hadn't even discussed who Hearts were up against. I peered out of the glass and noted that the opposition were in blue and white stripes. Not wanting to look stupid I decided not to ask who the other team were and quickly racked my brains to review the teams in the Premier League. Not Celtic, Rangers or Hibs obviously with this size crowd. Motherwell play in yellow, Dundee United in orange, Dundee all-blue, Kilmarnock… that was it, Killie!

Hearts started confidently and well they might because the Rugby Park side had made a poor fist of the early season. I knew enough to know that, unlike Hearts, they hadn't really established themselves firmly in the top flight and looking at the two line-ups it was the Jambos who had the internationals on view – Mackey, McPherson, Maclaren and Robertson. Even though I was distracted and concentrating on contacting Granville, I could soon see that the home side got into an easy rhythm and established control of the midfield.

It was no surprise that twenty minutes in Robertson found Joe Millar unmarked in the box and the little man stuck it in the corner. Soon after that, Maclaren came up for a corner and couldn't believe his luck when the keeper missed the cross and he got a free header from six yards. 2-0 and Tynecastle was rocking.

I focused and found Granville at the dugout.

"Hey, my old mate, nice to see you."

"Good evening," said Granville as though nothing had happened. His voice sounded weaker. He wasn't strong in reception. "Hello Catty, why is that ball with you not responding to me – he is blocking everything. Is he safe?"

"Yes," Catty replied "What's the low down in the dugout?"

"Well, pretty much as you'd expect. Alex Totten is tearing his hair out and Tommy McLean's well satisfied. Killie haven't got much firepower to bring off the bench but Totten wants to get them into the dressing room to get re-organised. McLean's just content to leave it as it is and you can't blame him."

I told Granville of the plan and he said okay. But he still had not worked out the aborigine bit of Josh's dream. We talked intermittently until half time. I also felt sorry for Gemma who had got us here, yet with no real proof of what was happening. So I scanned her mind through Granville and told her what she had been doing in her consultancy and even quoted phrases and financial figures. I asked her if she wanted anything from Chris's brain. She wanted to know the answer to one question to do with the take-overs. She was delighted and asked for one final bit of proof. What was she thinking at that very moment? I scanned and told her that she hoped for her private book review club to get some recognition. I gave her Granville's reply.

"Yes you will and you will be even mentioned in a novel!" She was converted.

I got up and said to Chris that I fancied going down and watching the second half from the stands and he would have nothing to do with it. He told me I couldn't get down there anyway because of security.

I was frantic! I turned to Catty and made some suggestions.

"Don't worry. I've just had a word with Granville and we have a better plan! Trust me." I did trust her so I went along with it.

The second half started but I wasn't concentrating that much, partly because the game seemed to be decided. Killie tightened things up a bit but they weren't making chances. Miserable stuff for their small bunch of fans in the 9,000 crowd. Some of them started to drift towards the exits when Mackey steamed through the middle to plant a third in the bottom corner. Three-goal comebacks in the last quarter are rare in anyone's book but for this team on this night, impossible. Hearts sensed the mood and they lacked urgency for the last fifteen minutes but the fans were reasonably happy though realistic – the real test was the Auld Firm. At least I had the added interest of listening in to the Scottish ball chants.

I prayed for the end of the game. It came and Gemma asked Chris if we could meet the players. He said yes. We waited for a while until the crowds had gone, then went down to the tunnel. At the end, players were mingling and coaches stood around chewing the fat of the game with an array of balls at their feet. I scanned for Granville. Third from the end. He said he would have to switch off as he was getting weak.

"What do we do?" I asked Catty.

"I am going to swap our friend with Granville – you and Alex create a distraction."

"Okay, he is third from the end and has switched off!"

Alex took charge and asked for everybody's attention (musicians are good at this). Gemma did a brilliant 'I am thick and would like to touch the balls' act whilst Catty moved the balls around a bit and did her swap.

"Lets go!" she said.

We exited quickly and called a taxi. Whilst we were waiting I held Granville and asked for acknowledgement. This strange voice said, "What the fuck are you doin, pal?"

We had got the wrong ball!!!!

I ran back in and found Chris walking towards the exit.

"Chris, sorry but I think I have dropped my dictaphone in the tunnel and we're leaving tomorrow!"

"Okay, let's go find it."

We walked to the tunnel and found the coaches muttering in disgust about something. I pretended to look for my lost property and scanned – no Granville!!

I quickly spun round when I heard one of the coaches saying he would like to get hold of the bastard that has just run off with a ball. Oh shit. I scanned the remaining balls for information.

"He's left a message for you," one said. "You have to follow him to the HOLY LOCH."

Chapter 9 – The Magnificent Seven

After a night of being both distraught and relieved that we had met Granville, we took stock and Gemma arranged for us to get a hire car. She furnished both Catty and me with food and maps and an array of phone numbers. Catty explained that she knew of the area and had no problems in driving there.

We thanked Alex and Gemma and promised to call in on our return to England. We left the stolen ball as Alex had promised to return him at the next local match.

We set off. Catty drove us out of Edinburgh; we took the route which was towards Glasgow then across the Clyde.

Catty explained that Ossie had told her he was happy to be swapped for Granville – partly to help us get him back because he realised we were Granvillle's friends, but also so that he could join the Hearts balls. After being constantly at the mercy of capricious children he was only too glad to be back in a professional environment where players treated balls with respect. We thought about him for a bit, a little sad not to have him with us anymore but he was in a good place.

Eventually we ended up in a tiny car park waiting for a ferry to cross the Clyde.

"There you are," said Catty. "That over there is the Holy Loch!"

It was a marvellous sight to look at.

The small ferry arrived. We pulled the car on and parked. It wasn't busy and the crossing was gentle and slow, so I got out of the car and stretched my legs.

I was starting to get really frustrated that I hadn't spoke to Granville for some time now. Yet I didn't feel upset about his demise, even though I wasn't sure what it was.

I then heard a voice saying, "Hey you! Yes you. Bring yer arse over here."

I looked around and casually looked in everyone's car, but couldn't find the ball.

"I'm here under the ropes and chains near the stairs." I mooched across and sat on the bottom of the stairs; there was a ball nestling in ropes and grease.

"What's happening?" I asked.

"Al tell ye – Ah been on this fucking ferry for six months noow. The skipper keeps me here fer when it's no busy. I'm mighty pissed o' wi' it I cannae tell you. He can't kick a ball – I spend half my time in the fucking Clyde swimming in seagull shite. GET ME AFF!!!"

"Does that mean you want me to rescue you?" I asked, thinking this is getting a bit regular.

"Onythin is better than seagull shite!"

"Okay, where would you like to go? Where do you come from?"

"I used to live in the dugout at Celtic Park and it was no picnic, let me tell ye. Ye ken that the Gers have been making all the runnin' of late?" I nodded and he carried on. "Well, every match for the Bhoys has become full o' tension and there's jist no enjoyment there at a'. All the balls have picked up the atmosphere and there's nae chanting, or jokes, nothin'. I dinna want to go back there, pal!"

"Okay, indulge me," I responded. "But first, has the ball Granville Tingate passed this way? And then tell me of your experiences – you know some Rangers/Celtic stuff."

"Aye, he came through last night but he was awfee weak. Take to the north side of the Holy Loch, but be careful mind, there are some powerful Celts oot there!"

"Are they violent?"

"Dina worry aboot yer body – it's yer mind. Ah'll be away there when ah finish ma time but no' yet."

"Let's talk football."

"Okay, I'll tell ye what ah ken. You think you know about derby games because you've been to some in England. Man, they canna compare. Boil down centuries of hatred and put it in a football match and that's the Auld Firm game. Even yon English brought in by Souness get affected by it. That Terry Butcher comes up from sleepy Suffolk and starts behaving as if he's been banging a Lambeg drum in a flute band all his life. It worked though because the Gers are dominant now and they're attracting better players than Celtic, so they could be on top for years.

Me? Well I get bored by it all tae be honest. I would have enjoyed the Eighties if I'd been around 'cos Aberdeen and Dundee United broke their grip but that's over now. And now we never do the business in Europe do we? Time was when Rangers and Celtic were challenging for trophies abroad but that's all over."

He carried on lamenting the state of the Scottish domestic game and all those matches on the Celtic bench had given him a profoundly pessimistic outlook. Mind you, daily dips in seagull shite can't have helped.

We reached the pier at Hunter's Quay. We took the ball along the road to the castle and left him there in the grounds. I think he wanted to laird it over the town. I asked for some direction and he said to try anyone with an understanding of Gaelic as he was sure things happened somewhere round here to do with strange customs. Catty and I walked for a while and she explained that the football ground here was called the Black Park but she didn't know why. Also I was informed that the Cowal Highland Games were held here in August and the main street was filled with pipers – moving up and down all day getting very drunk. She also talked about the puffers (little steamboats) that used to sail up and down the Clyde and pull into the coal pier.

We carried on to the end of the high street, which was called Argyle Street, and I was given a quick lesson in spelling i.e. Argyle is a street in Glasgow and Argyll is the county we are in now.

We wound up and down two or three streets not daring to ask people what would seem stupid questions, and then I spied a little brown shop with what I thought was a Gaelic sign. It said "Dae It Yersel". Catty shouted to hold on, but I was already in the shop asking if the man spoke Gaelic. He said yes and carried on with his shopkeeping.

I then plucked up courage and said, do you know anything about the history of footballs around here. He asked why. So I coughed and stuttered, trying to say I was undertaking studies of football movements, which sounded pathetic.

Catty jumped in and saved me by saying, "I understand there is a practising Celt at the north side of the Holy Loch who can answer our questions – do you know who he is?"

"Och no," came the reply, then he leaned across the counter and wiggled his finger for us to come closer. "Every two weeks at midday there is a man that comes from the north called Oor Wullie. He kens about these things and might help ye. You'll find him at the botanical gardens at the bottom of loch Eck – at the north-east side of the loch. He always takes some time there before crossing to

Glasgie." He went back to his shopkeeping and that was that. If we asked more questions he just shook his head.

We left and took a short ride in the car to find the botanical gardens. Catty pointed out that the shop name 'Dae it yersel' was simply 'do it yourself', a little DIY shop.

We arrived at the gardens and went in, and waited in a seating area.

We checked everyone out as they came in and no one was ball psychic, until a wee man with white hair and a smile as wide as the Clyde came strolling over. He looked at home. In fact he was the type of person that would look at home anywhere. He came and greeted us formally and asked where we had come from. He had eyes that saw into your very soul.

We answered cordially.

He put his hands in his pockets, grinned and said, "I know this is a personal question but do you have a ball for me. You see, every now and then people give me balls to take on my journey. Please don't be offended by my request as you may be the wrong people and not who I'm looking for."

We sat there open mouthed and both felt we were in the presence of someone who had been there and done it all twenty times.

I replied quickly and started to explain the situation.

He raised his hand gently and said, "Is your ball already with Tam?"

I told him about Granville being abducted at the Hearts ground. "Aye that'll be Tam. Look I'm a bit behind time in my travels so could you take the other six balls to Tam for me. He'll no hurt you if you have the other six!"

"Is there something special about the other six?"

"Well to me there is. I don't talk to them or anything like

that but ever since I was young I seem to be attracted to balls left by the wayside and occasionally I steal balls from their owners if I get the urge. It seems crazy but I deliver them to Tam who is always looking for his magical seven. Occasionally I deliver to a blond-haired lady up north called Morag. Tam says it's to do with the old ways, far back past what anyone can remember. All I know is that I feel I am doing a service to the ball and the land. I can't explain. Tam once tried but I couldn't take what he was saying seriously. Yet, I still do it. Anyway I've got to be on my way."

He told us how to get to Tam and I asked, "Is he dangerous and has he got a gun?"

Wullie laughed and said, "Tam couldnae hit a bull on the arse wi' a tambourine even if it was stuck in a barn door."

"Well what do you mean by he won't hurt you?"

"Well, he has this way about him a bit like a panda. He is very gentle and sensitive but you always have the feeling that he could be incredibly aggressive and merciless if needed, and he tunes in to you, and has the measure of you before you can blink."

We thanked Wullie and decide to stay in the gardens with the six balls as Tam would not be back until evening. Wullie told us he was off to his next call – he was a travelling salesman for wool and fabrics. He was totally pissed off at all the tourist shops purporting to have quality mohair when, according to Wullie, you could drive a horse and cart through the picks.

We talked for a while and then said our goodbyes. We took the six balls deep into the gardens and sat amongst them giving our introductions and pleasantries.

After our introductions it seemed that the balls were fading fast and were at the end of their time. They didn't know where they were being taken but just knew it was right for them. They informed us that the Catty and myself types were often chosen as deliverers. Being more specific, to record their last sayings and experiences.

It made sense as Wullie told us that all tides around Britain push in a clockwise direction. Therefore the balls had come from Ireland, Wales, and England, and even could come from South America or the Caribbean. One ball informed me that when the Scots go down to Scarborough in summer by the droves, their secret mission is to get the balls back that have been pushed down the coastline.

We took paper and pens from the car and settled in for an afternoon of recording their last thoughts and memories.

The six balls we met were: Rivelino, a ball that had travelled all the way from South America. He was on extremely good terms with Viv Richards, the other ball that had travelled a huge distance, coming all the way from the Caribbean. Next to these two was a ball that never seemed to stop talking although we got him to calm down enough to tell us his name – Emlyn Hughes from Liverpool. Listening to this lot sounded like a meeting of the United Nations because also in there were Ian McDonald, who as might be expected was Scottish, and a ball with a distinct Irish lilt named Liam Brady. Finally there was one ball that didn't really join in the general banter but told us he was known as Clockwork Ocwirk!

I asked Catty if she knew why he would be called that but she just shrugged and looked blank. As Clockwork didn't seem inclined to furnish an explanation I left it and spoke to Viv Richards.

"Why does a football take the name of a cricketer then?" I asked.

"Because I is an Antiguan ball, man," he drawled, "and King Vivvy is a hero to the whole island. Plus, Vivvy once put his boots on to play for the boys in the World Cup qualifiers, so there it is."

They all had plenty to say and because we couldn't get their thoughts if they all kept on at the same time, they agreed to settle down and speak in turn. Granville had told them that we would write down their thoughts for posterity. First off was Rivelino, who spoke English surprisingly well and was full of stories about South American soccer and how dangerous it can be for balls.

"Fans have been known to shoot balls you know," he said, "and they stab them too if an argument starts. Kick a ball over a person's garden fence in Brasil and there's every chance it won't come back."

"But then there's the excitement." Rivelino started to warm to his theme. "The skill and touch of the players, the way they really appreciate a ball and what you can do with it. I'm named after the great exponent of the banana shot, but I've never been kicked by him personally though," he added regretfully.

"Those that have talk about the experience in truly glowing terms. Here was a player who was a prince among ball psychics. But there's so many others, even those who never played the game professionally, who really love the ball and treat it accordingly."

"Why do the South Americans feel so fanatical about soccer?" asked Catty.

"Well, for some of the answers you must look to poverty, because soccer is a game you can play anywhere with minimum equipment. Then there is the passion in the Latin people and the influence of the immigrants. And the desire for new countries with few resources to be proud and recognised in the world; in some cases soccer is all that puts us on the map. Haven't you heard the phrase 'Uruguay isn't a country, it's a football team'?"

We had to admit that that particular phrase had passed us by.

"Finally there is the Latin American psyche," continued Rivelino. "That machismo that fuels the males and makes them do crazy things like bullfights and duels and the like. One respected Argentinian writer says that in South American culture, football has replaced the knife fight as an expression of male virility. That explains why some of our players have been a little over-aggressive," he added with some understatement.

What he was saying chimed in with a lot of the history and analysis Granville gave me a few weeks ago.

"Man, that Vivvy, he's just the same," interjected Viv. "When he went out to bat for the Windies he said it was the same as being in a war, fighting for your country. He's a warrior determined to show no fear to those rapid guys – no helmet for the King, no way. I understand you, bro'," he said to Rivelino.

Viv's life as a ball was very different from his companion's. Soccer being very much a beach pastime in the Caribbean, he spent a lot of time in lazy beach games and because so many people either forgot him or kicked him out to sea by accident, Viv had floated to almost all the islands at least once. As a result he had developed an exceptionally laid-back view of the world, although he did regret that he wouldn't be in Jamaica in a couple of years time.

"I won't have the chance to go to the World Cup in France 98 with the Reggae Boyz, and I know they will qualify!" he said mournfully.

While we were chatting, both Catty and I were aware of Emlyn Hughes chattering away in the background desperate to be at the centre of the conversation. When we weren't attentive enough he tried to engage with 'Clockwork' who chose to be completely indifferent to Emlyn's banter. We turned our attention to Ian McDonald.

"I'm from close by compared to these lads," he said referring to Rivelino and Viv. "From Stranraer to be exact. Do you know it?" We nodded and Catty said she had once caught the ferry to Ireland from there.

"That's how I got here," interjected Liam Brady, "but I'll let Ian carry on and tell you about me in a minute."

"Aye, well we're more well known for that than anything the football team's achieved. I'm named after the player with most League appearances for the club. There have never been any internationals at Stranraer but we do go back a long way because the club was founded in 1870."

It was interesting chatting to Ian but I didn't think he'd be able to tell us anything amazing. He must have guessed what I was thinking. He spluttered out quickly.

"I know the difference between a mickle, muckle and a pickle and a puckle – do you?"

I was completely lost and thought, you have really caught me out.

"This applies to anything you know – for example a piece of cake. Pickle means less than a half, puckle means just less than normal size, mickle means just more than normal size, and muckle means fucking big!" I made notes.

He said, feeling confident that he had my attention again, "I haven't spent all my time in Stranraer though. I've been up and down the west coast and up to the big city. I belonged to a salesman who worked the area and carried me round in his car boot. In fact he had two stickers in the back windscreen of the car which said 'Careful, balls on board' and 'Balls aren't just for Christmas, they are for life'. Every so often he'd pull me out for kickabouts and I met lots of other balls during the journeys. I picked up dozens and dozens of ball sea shanties during my travels and I need you to write them down. Listen, I've picked up loads from all round the coastline of Britain. Here's a good one from Grimsby…

– Four score and ten balls and men...we're bound for Grimsby town...

Or a more rude one…
– We were on the good ship Venus
– By hell you should have seen us
– The balls didn't care for trifles
– They rolled round the deck
– Playing merry eck
– And someone would shoot them with rifles
– The first ball's name was Cropper
– By hell he wasn't a flopper
– He would roll twice round the deck
– Roll twice round someone's neck
– Then up the nearest arse for a stopper!"

Liam Brady joined in the singing and said how much he enjoyed listening to Ian. Liam had only recently ended up on the Scottish coast; he'd been booted overboard during a ferry crossing and drifted in with the tide. A little boy found him and took him home but had lost him in the Paisley area and eventually through many adventures he had found his way to this group. What was most interesting about Liam though was that originally he wasn't a soccer ball but a Gaelic football.

"Then someone gave me away to a friend of his who put me in a jumble sale. Someone bought me and they used me for a soccer ball after that. I can still remember being used for the Gaelic game though; it's a great game for a ball because you get so much variety. They punt you long distances like in rugby, have shots like in football, bounce you like a basketball and have a hand-pass like in handball. I never ever got bored I can tell you."

Liam was getting excited now. He continued. "You know Australian Rules Football developed from Gaelic Football?"

I'd heard something about that but nothing specific, so I asked him to go on.

"Yes, it was the Irish who moved there in the early days for the gold prospecting. They even play international matches, Ireland v Australia, with rules that combine the two games. They're both about as aggressive as each other anyway."

Liam was full of funny and odd stories about the game but his best one was the first-ever Australian Rules game under organised laws. Now, even today Aussie Rules is played on the biggest pitch of all football games but that's nothing compared to the early days. The very first match was played on an area that had the goals a mile apart and 40 on each side! They had agreed that the winning side would be the first to score two but by nightfall the score was still only 1-0. They had to come back and continue a fortnight later and everyone sort of realised that changes were needed to make it more exciting.

Liam continued by saying that his other claim to fame was that he knew all the television adverts and used to spend many happy hours setting quizzes to other balls in the locker rooms. He shared a few difficult ones.

"Right, you finish the advert. The first one is: light up the sky with…?"

I knew it from years ago but couldn't finish it with

words. I could sing it but it just didn't come to the front of my brain.

"How about this one then: 1001 cleans a big big carpet for…? Or… For hands that do dishes stay soft as your face with mild…? Or… Tastes good – looks good and…? Or… Murraymints, murraymints too good…?"

He went through dozens, and we all felt inadequate and kept repeating the first part in the vain hope the last words would pop out.

By the time we had all of Liam's many stories and adverts down, Emlyn was absolutely bursting to be at the centre of the action. He proved to be hyperactive, unable to stay on one point for any length of time and full of chants. They just flowed out of him in an endless stream and he always finished every rendition with the phrase, 'Good one eh? Good one.' Of all the balls, he reminded me of the young ones Granville had pointed out when we went to the Villa-Newcastle game.

Coming from a soccer-mad city like Liverpool he had met all sorts of other balls influenced by the soccer passions of the three teams on Merseyside. He was very keen to make it clear that we shouldn't forget Tranmere Rovers. All in all it could be very wearing trying to keep up with Emlyn, especially when he started on his ball versions of Shakespeare.

"A ball, a ball, my kingdom for a ball! A goal, a goal, my kitbag for a goal! Good one 'eh? Is this a goal-mouth I see before me? Or what about – All the world's a ball and we are merely players? Good one!"

He told me that the first football chant was written by the poet Byron. "He banged the leather for goal." He then punctuated his declamatory verse with many chants and even Christmas carols, including…

"Oh score all ye faithful,
I'm dreaming of a round Christmas,
We three balls of orient are,
I saw three balls come sailing in,
Away in a stadium… no chance of a goal, and
Whiz-bang boot it up on high, the balls in heaven are scoring.

Whiz-bang let the volleys fly, the goals will not be boring"

Other one-liners were:

Is that a whistle in your pocket or are you going to book me?

Who shoots wins.

It's not the balls in my life, it's the life in my balls!

Why, why, why touch-linesman.

Shall all the perfumes in sweet Arabia ne'er sweeten this goalie's armpit?

Pink Floyd 'Dark side of the ball'."

I remembered talking to the rugby balls at Murrayfield and tittered to myself at the one they sang me. You know the old Bob Marley favourite – 'No Irvine, no try; No Irvine, no try'.

Finally we had copious notes about Emlyn's stuff and moved on to the serene Clockwork Ocwirk. We introduced ourselves and asked where he came from and where he got such a name.

"So you do not know where it comes from?" he asked. We shook our heads.

"If I tell you that for many years I belonged to the grandchildren of an Austrian scientist who came to this country as a very young man soon after World War Two, does that help?"

"Not really, I'm afraid."

"Call yourself a football fan," he snorted. "Look, in the 1930s the Austrian team were considered the greatest in the world, called the 'Wunderteam'. They only didn't win the 1938 World Cup because their best players ended up in the German team. After the war another great team was built and they got to the semi-finals of the 1954 World Cup. Before that they caused a stir by drawing 2-2 at Wembley in 1951 – remember England were considered invincible at home in those days.

"Star of that side was the defender Ernst Ocwirk, known as 'Clockwork'. He was so good he went to Italy to play professionally there and he was the soccer hero of the old gentleman who used to tell his grandkids all about Clockwork Ocwirk."

"Well thank you for that," said Catty with a trace of irony.

"Not at all," replied Clockwork, who was a ball who appeared to be quite full of himself. It turned out that this was because of his contact with the old Professor who, in the manner of many a genius according to Granville, had been ball psychic. Over several years they had discussed scientific and philosophical matters far removed from Emlyn's crude ball chants.

Clockwork was the opposite of Rivelino who talked in mystical language about the swerve and spin imparted to a ball by great players. This erudite ball preferred to see it all in terms of physics and aeronautics. He launched into a learned treatise on the subject, which included reference to the way a ball travels at altitude.

"This explains the efficiency of the free-kicks taken at the Mexico World Cup," he explained. "Less resistance through the air and goalkeepers uncertain of their angles and the trajectory in these unfamiliar conditions."

He touched a raw nerve here. Rivelino was dismissive enough of Clockwork's theories even before he started applying them to Brazil's finest hour; he hit the roof when his great hero's skills were questioned.

"So what about the ratio of long shots at the 1978 Mundial? The goals by Haan, Brandts, Nelinho eh? No altitude there!"

"Of course, if a considerable number of strikes are made from outside the box, random theory indicates that a proportionate amount will travel to the target and beyond the goalkeeper." I detected a patronising and slightly weary tone to Clockwork's voice.

"You have no soul!" exclaimed Rivelino.

"Quite possibly," agreed Clockwork, "but the existence of a godlike entity and metaphysical rebirth is not the subject we are discussing. Also, I have dreams just like anyone else – they are just a little more outlandish. I used to look up at the stars on a clear night and consider the universe and possible parallel universes. I would consider where the first sphere came from. Was the big bang theory correct? Or was there a big ball-shaped mass that exploded into trillions of smaller balls or spheres. I, like most intelligent balls, would think that in the beginning there was the ball, and all other balls were created in seven days. I think lots of balls would like to finish their time by being a shooting star.

"But consider the permutations of other universes. They are infinite. There is bound to be a galaxy made up of planet-sized footballs. Also knowing that most galaxies lie along a flat elliptical plane (not unlike a football stadium) there could be giant football goalposts at either end. As the planets move around and get into the goal-mouth they would explode as supernovas and turn into negative matter and reappear as positive matter at some point elsewhere on the pitch – keeping the galaxy game going for eternity.

"Now that would make our game interesting for the fans, wouldn't it? The fans could put on bets as to where it would appear. The odds would be good for the ball to reappear on the foot of a player. Just think of the betting odds at the bookies. Or how many matches it would take before the ball reappears on the penalty spot?"

"Having said that, I'm not crazy like some balls that believe they have been abducted by aliens – that's childish. Their stories are so transparent; they always say, I was on the way home in a team bus when there was a blinding flash of light, then they would find themselves in a space ship. They always saw the spaceship full of weird shaped grey balls – then would wake up back at the team locker room – pathetic! And of course, all space ships are ball shaped."

I stepped in there, just as Rivelino was about to explode, even though I was curious to see how balls could engineer a physical confrontation. Catty took Rivelino to one side and she and Vivvy calmed him down, leaving me with the seemingly oblivious Clockwork. While I shared the Brazilian ball's romanticism, I was nevertheless fascinated by his antagonist, and his theories.

Clockwork went on to explain to me that balls are very rarely completely stationary – being spheroids they obviously are built for circulatory motion and that being so, it often proves very difficult for them to disobey their natures. For a soccer ball this can mean having to develop self-control, particularly in windy conditions. If you are the average ball sat in the garden it matters not if you oscillate pleasurably in the gentle breeze – everyone expects it. But if you're in the middle of a match and can't control it then the consequences can be massive. As an example he explained that balls on the penalty spot cannot afford to move even a millimetre in case it affected the strike. He sympathised even more with golf balls who are expected to preserve perfect stillness in windy conditions on slick surfaces offering minimal grip. One of his more humorous lines was that he once had a recurring nightmare, which was that he woke up to find he had been turned into a glass marble.

"You see Alan Shepherd understood that," he mused.

"The astronaut?"

"Yes exactly." I detected a note of surprise and respect in Clockwork's voice. "When he took the golf ball for that shot on the moon he placed a ball in a perfect situation – a shot hit without any wind and minimal gravity, one where a ball can roll to its maximum ability without hindrance – total kinetic momentum. To be that ball…"

It was comforting to find that Clockwork experienced dreams just like Rivelino but sad that the scientific one could never achieve his while the Brazilian's could be waiting for him on any field, every day.

Chapter 10 – Shapeshifting

We then set off to meet Tam MacAulay. We were told to head down the north side of the Holy Loch and stop just after the Kirk of Kilmun. We did and walked a few yards to find a forest road stretching high up into the hills. We started walking and left the balls in the car. After only a few yards it was amazing; you couldn't hear anything but the rain and wind in the trees. Catty said that when it gets dark there, there is still a strange light. Everything is soft and springy underfoot. You can only smell wet tree, nutmeg and cinnamon.

We were coming to a brow where it seemed like the whole view of the Clyde opened up in front of us. Then a small stocky man came walking towards us. We knew it was Tam! He walked with purpose towards us. He was tanned and windswept with long flowing, curly dark hair. He had an axe in one hand and fastened to his waist was a bag made out of netting with a ball inside. He stopped ten yards away with an expressionless look, never took his eyes off us, and said,

"Are these the ones?"

"Yes, these are my little pixies," came thundering into our heads from Granville!

"Granville!" we both exclaimed and ran towards him. Tam loosened his grip on the axe, sat down on the forest road edge and freed Granville from the bag. I just wanted to boot him all the way down the forest road. Catty was almost shrieking questions at him. He was answering with his usual calm collected self.

Then Tam interrupted, seeming agitated.

"Where are the other six?" I told him they were in the car at the bottom of the forest road.

"Give me the keys," he said with urgency. I gave them to him and he started off down the road.

"See you in five minutes," he demanded. We nodded.

"Well," said Granville. "How do you like Scotland, Bren?"

"I'm learning!"

"Did you think about the possibilities of what it might be like?"

"No. I need more practice."

"Well, bless you, you have the rest of your life."

"What's next?" Catty chipped in.

"It's a long story! But I'll shorten the facts – as you know I haven't got long to go. The reason is that if you squeeze me you'll find less air inside me than before. It's quite simple. The other six have the same problem – some of old age and some have been punctured."

"Punctured!" I exclaimed in disbelief, "I thought you were invincible."

"No, just like you, we all have to go sometime. You humans are nothing more than wobbly jellies and a bone structure. Very vulnerable I would say. Anyway, were you expecting some great finish? It's not going to happen in terms of my demise. What will be unique is the finish this night. I am privileged to know about this place and soon we will go a little further to shapeshift."

"Shapeshift? Where are we going?"

"Up a hillside not too far from here. It took me a while to work out the possibilities of the dreamer's dream of aborigine designs, but I got it in the end. At the bottom of

Kilmartin valley are a series of hills but first I want you to take me to crown me temporary king of Dalriada."

"What!" I said staring across the Clyde.

"I know where," said Catty, "You're looking in the wrong direction. We are going to take the balls up Dunaad."

"Quite right, my dear," answered Granville. "I will not upset the Scots as I only want to be king for two minutes. But it will add to my life story when you tell it. We are losing time and the others will be waiting. Tonight is the last night."

We took Granville back down the hill to meet Tam who was engrossed in conversation with the balls.

"Right. C'mon," said Tam jumping into the car. "We must complete everything by the time the moon rises over the cup and rings."

Catty knew where she was going and Tam spoke to me.

"Everything that is about to happen is for your eyes only. You are both honoured to be here – not for me but for the balls and especially the Big Ball (he meant Granville – just the way they say Big Man in Scotland). Legends are always allowed a little extra, so he is to be crowned king ball of Dalriada for two minutes. You will see later. After, we have to climb a hill to the cup and rings, which could be mistaken for aborigine designs. That is where we say goodbye to our ball friends.

My family have been doing this for years with balls and other inanimate objects. There are too many secrets to say why this happens and we – there are more like me – have handed the secrets down through the generations. Just watch and join in and enjoy." I shuddered and thought, 'I do not want to cross this man'.

We drove for just over an hour and ended up at the bottom end of Kilmartin valley where there is a hill that stands on its own. It looked like nothing special or different. I could understand why people would simply drive past unless they knew about it. But when we climbed it, it felt like I was walking into the past. Sensations and feelings roared inside of me. It was a hill fort where the Dalriadic kingdom of the Scots ruled from way back in the 5th century.

We sat at the top and talked of the view and its history. Tam would have kept us there all night if it were not for the urgency to be up at the cup and rings.

Granville was placed on a slab near the top where there is a footprint in the stone. Tam placed a rowan branch at his left side and pointed a metal object that resembled a short sword at his right. Granville then said,

"I will uphold the honour of the kingdom."

Then Tam added, "Lead your people and balls with pride and integrity," as he poured water from the stony bowl beside the slab onto Granville's much marked skin.

Granville being crowned, we left and the balls all had a great conversation of how people may remember Granville as the king for a while, but how many would remember the six members of his temporary clan?

We all left and followed Tam's instructions to find the cup and rings. We parked and set off up a steep climb, which brought us out onto the top of a hill area overlooking the most green and brown valleys.

There were some slabs laying flat in the grass and Tam declared we had arrived. The slabs had indents that were circular – some small and some large. I tried to make sense of them. Are they planets and constellations? Or like the aborigine's marks of families and where they live in relation to the valleys. There were a series of lines crossing through the rings.

Tam poured water into the indents and sat down.

"Place the balls where they want and move them if they ask to be moved. Some balls will switch off for a time but don't worry about it." Tam took out a flask of whisky and first sprinkled it lightly on the slabs and then took a throatful.

"Okay we can relax and talk now."

I asked Tam about the tides that Oor Wullie mentioned and he said that Britain and Europe were full of ancient sites and that balls could seek them out by taking the coastal or inland water route. He said that even today as in olden times water was the best way to travel.

"What about all the London balls?" I asked. He said that he'd heard a lot of them head for Cornwall or Brittany in France – full of ancient sites.

Tam talked of many things and the balls joined in. We were glad that Tam had told us to buy some food and bring blankets up the hill as darkness was now setting in.

The moon appeared and placed itself in all the cups and rings. It was a magical site. The balls looked like giant round globes on a sea of rocks and small moon-glowing lakes.

I thought of the first night when I met Granville – the moon in the cobbled street. I thought of the rat and looked directly in front of me – about twenty feet away two rats were looking at me. They almost bowed and turned to be on their way.

We talked until the early hours of just about every subject you could imagine. Also every football team came up. Tam did not know any football facts in terms of matches, but he knew of all the reasons why strange things happened at matches. Here are some of them that he related.

He told us about the balls bursting in the 1946 and 1947

cup finals. At the time this was described as a million-to-one chance but in fact it was planned. The balls that were used for those finals had been around for some time. Like the professional footballers their careers had been cut short by the war because they hadn't been lucky enough to be used in any of the wartime internationals and their outings had been limited to kickabouts by the FA members who were not on war service.

As a result when the chance came for the big one, they agreed that as many of them should get a chance as possible. The only way to do this was for the chosen ball to sacrifice itself and so allow the second ball to take the stage. By doing this four balls went out in a blaze of glory instead of two.

Tam had also heard tales about the famous 1966 ball, the one they played with in the World Cup Final. Amazingly, this most famous leather had been spirited away to Germany after the game by a German fan who caught it as it was kicked into the crowd at the climax. Apparently, this ball remained adamant that he had crossed the line for the third goal, a fact that he communicated at the time to the ball psychic Russian linesman.

He also knew about some amazing goals. One was from the time that boots had metal toecaps. A Burnley player hit the ball so hard that his toecap came off – the ball was shocked to see the cap heading goalward but even more surprised when the goalie saved the said item while the ball trickled into the net laughing its head off.

Some of Granville's last words were about how I should proceed in life. I asked about whether or not I should follow my sports writer idea.

"It's up to you. You can do anything you like if you count backwards!"

"Count backwards?" I asked.

"Yes. Simply close your eyes and imagine you are going down in a lift and count backwards slowly from level twenty to zero and imagine you have just contacted your subconscious. Tell your subconscious what you want or imagine it happening. Then move the lift up to level five and repeat your desire. Then move the lift up to level ten and repeat again. Then come up the lift to level twenty and open your eyes and carry on with your day. Do this four or five times a day and slowly you will start to achieve what you want."

"It's that simple is it?"

"Yes, I used to call it the toilet method for humans. If you undertake this short exercise every time you go to the loo – that'll be, enough. It should take only about the same time as it takes to undertake your ablutions."

"Okay, I'll try it."

"But be careful. Because if you start getting what you want you will change and people around you will have their constructs of you destroyed. I have seen many relationships broken because people change."

"Well, how do constructs work and what is a good relationship?"

"Constructs are the mental subconscious predictions you make just before something happens. At its most simplistic – imagine you go home on a dark evening and switch the light on and the bulb has gone. Well, you have imagined the room lit and the light working for a millisecond before it happens and that is why you get a shock, and are lost for a few seconds. Take that on to the pitch and footballers that rely on their constructs to get through a game will constantly give them shocks. But the subconscious works faster if you implant perfection. Just think of some players who have had their constructs wrong when the ball does not go in the net – and the disappointment.

I thought of Jeff Astle, forever frozen in the memories of a particular generation of Englishmen (and Scots but with more fondness) missing an oh-so-easy chance against Brazil in the 1970 World Cup game. He only played once more for his country and that was in the same tournament. And Gordon Smith, one on one with the Man Utd keeper in the last minute of an FA Cup Final to win it for Brighton – he must have dreamt about being in that situation since before he even became a professional and now it's really all we remember him for.

"Too many players do not know when to rely on their implanted subconscious skills rather than constructs or consciousness. It's sometimes a reflection of bad training. For example if you had a novice player, young, but with potential; when practising for the score they should start by scoring from simple angles with the goal keeper positioned for ease of scoring and gradually increase the difficulty. The first time he misses, you go back to simple until his subconscious has built up a habit, for want of a better word, of never missing. He does not need to think on the pitch then – he simply puts it in from everywhere, everytime."

"And relationships?"

"It's not up to me to say what is good or bad, but I can tell you this. Your personality as Bren is made up of values. For example you may value football, a good curry, honesty, fair play and being on your own, etc. Normally an ordinary adult operates on about two thousand of these. Some are used every day and some come out now and then. A relationship is dependent on either agreeing or putting up with each others values, because that's what makes you different from, for example, Catty."

"Yes, but we have been getting on famously and now you're making it sound like we are very different."

"You have been getting on whilst you have been chasing me because you have only brought to the surface a few of your values. Why not get a note pad sometime and write down all the things you value, even down to your favourite piece of music. Ask Catty to do the same and you can spend the next two years working out if you are compatible. Most people try long preliminary relationships but unfortunately never bring all of the values out. Ten years later a situation occurs which raises suppressed values and bingo – a hell of a disagreement."

I thought of Catty and me and watched her talking to the balls and Tam. She looked so happy and full of life. I thought about how her values might be different from mine and how that would affect my constructs. Start simple, I thought, and make it perfect every time. If something happens then go back a little in the relationship until it is perfect. Great.

Granville suggested that we all get a little sleep as it was a long night. We shut our eyes for what seemed like two minutes.

I awoke to find Tam standing at the edge of the slabs, staring out on a misty morning over the valleys as though looking for something in the distance.

"You okay, Tam?"

"Aye, just looking for what's going to happen next – it's a new day."

I'd thought of more things to ask Granville whilst I was dozing. So I turned, and he was GONE! So were the other balls.

"Where have you put them, Tam?" I quizzed.

"I haven't moved them; they have shapeshifted into the

cup and rings," he said as though it happened every day.

I got up and moved over to the slabs. I started to count the cup and rings as I had done yesterday. There were more than yesterday, I thought.

"Which one is Granville?"

"Don't bother looking – it's all over and done with. Wake up Catty and we'll head down the valley."

I woke Catty up and told her what had happened.

"I know. I sort of woke up earlier and saw only two balls left on the slab. They were the colour of white brilliant chalk and seemed to get smaller and smaller – then I fell asleep again."

Tam encouraged us to leave as soon as possible. He wanted the hillside left to itself.

We walked down the hillside, and the mist cleared to reveal a glorious sun-splattering day. We warmed through quickly. As we reached the bottom I turned to speak to Tam. He had gone. I scanned the landscape and it seemed like he too had disappeared into thin air. We walked downwards and Catty pointed to the sky – seven shooting stars – one after the other. We looked at each other and said nothing. We reached the road at the bottom.

Catty asked me, "What now?"

I answered as best as I could. "Let's go find somewhere to have a nice cup of tea and talk about the possibilities!"

Chapter 11 – Postscript

This all happened a few years ago. I now spend my days thinking and writing and pretty much do what I like. It takes great effort to sit and think of possibilities that one has in one's life.

I still see my old friends. But they think that I spend too much time thinking and are constantly telling me that I have much to say and should write it down. Well, that's easy for them to say, but there are still too many possibilities, and I am always out of batteries for the dictaphone.

When I do decide to make a move, I make it, and usually shock my friends. They say things like, 'I can't see where you're coming from; where did that idea come from?' I usually reply with, 'I don't know where I'm coming from but I know where I am going up to a certain point because the possibilities start taking over.' This usually creates a conversation stopper and Phil's blood still drains from his face when I say things like that.

Even though I know where the dreamer is and see him when I visit Phil, I always keep the conversation simple and avoid asking about his dreams.

Yes, I still see Phil and good old Danny and I collected a fair amount of money from the predictions during the great monopoly game. They generously gave me the winnings that should have gone to Granville. Phil is still my big friend in life and Danny – he is really well known now for his predictability in sports – but we know where he gets that from, don't we?

No, I didn't end up with Catty. We took everything seriously and worked out what would happen with our values. We both agreed that we would impose too many differences on each other. I still see her from time to time. She has made a name for herself in the game at director level. I cannot say any more than that otherwise you will seek her out and ask too many questions.

I understand Alex found Morag on his secret travels to do with the Stone of Destiny in Scotland. Apparently she is also a writer and plays alto saxophone. They get on well and Gemma has had her book club put in glowing lights.

I have never seen Tam again but have heard stories of him 'repelling invaders' as he used to say.

Jimmy Hill is still in the rafters and others like Pongo Wareing are still there to this day. Joe Pepper did get back to York and when I go there on the train I have fleeting conversations with him. I went to watch Newcastle a few more times over the next couple of years because they still played exciting stuff; Tosh was on the bench for most of them but then I went to a game and couldn't contact him. Another ball explained that Tosh had been attacked by a dog and was mangled beyond repair – at least it happened on the Newcastle training pitch where he spent so much of his time.

As for Ossie, well he still stammers but not quite as badly. Surprisingly, he's had the most amazing adventures and is still having them now – he even went to a garden party at Buckingham Palace where he met a very important ball psychic but he won't tell anyone exactly who it was. 'It's a s-secret' he usually says.

As I said, I do work hard at thinking about many things and have found that I have changed. I am known to be a bit of a guru in many things. When I am not writing I sometimes help with literacy skills in schools for children with special educational needs.

I find that most will talk about any possibility and will show great enthusiasm in following your line of thought and developing it in all directions. They always will talk about football, both males and females. So when they ask me how I learnt to write, I always start by sitting them down comfortably with a football in their hands and tell them a story. It always starts with:

'It was one of those nights that I will never forget – standing outside in hard driving rain, a cold wind tearing into my very bones. Feet wet and sodden through, and the only protection I had was a small plastic bag with a change of socks, knickers and T-shirt. I wanted to curl up and put myself into the bag for a couple of hours…'